Lilacs & Lavender

By Zoe Burton

Lilacs & Lavender

ISBN: 978-1-953138-31-6

Acknowledgements

First, I thank Jesus Christ, my Savior and Guide, without whom this story would not have been told. I love you!

Additional thanks go to my betas, cold readers, and proof readers, Rose, Sarah B, Fa, Kathryn, and Debra. You stretched me and kept me on the straight and narrow, writing-wise. You rock!!

And special thanks to Leenie and Rose, and to all my Patreon Patrons. <3

Chapter 1

Meryton, Hertfordshire

Early December

The main street of Meryton was relatively quiet on this cold December morning as Elizabeth Bennet and her four sisters walked from their home, Longbourn, towards their Aunt Philips' house in the nearby town of Meryton.

Concern for her eldest sibling kept Elizabeth at Jane's side, their arms linked as the two walked behind the other three. Kitty and Lydia, being the youngest of the five, were eagerly anticipating the soldiers they hoped to run into in town, the redcoats the topic of their discussion. Mary, the middle sister, was attempting to read, and therefore frequently walked into her sisters or stumbled over the ruts in the roadway. The eldest two were more subdued. Jane, older by two years than Elizabeth, was struggling with unrequited love. Elizabeth strolled next to her, supportively holding her arm.

Just as they reached their aunt's door, chaos exploded across the way. All five Bennet sisters stopped and turned, staring in shock at what was happening.

There in the street was the milliner's youngest daughter in front of the shop, screaming at the top of her lungs at the middle daughter of the butcher. Each young lady was kicking, screaming, scratching, and biting. It appeared from the Bennets' point of view that there was hair pulling happening, as well. The sound of clothing being ripped added to the excitement.

"You baggage! What do you think you were doing with my George? He will never marry you! He is promised to me!" Miss Smith screamed as she kicked her adversary in the leg.

"Me a baggage? You are a tart! Throwing yourself at my betrothed! I know you are in the family way; I heard it at the grocer's a few minutes ago. Do you think to trap him? He will never marry you!" Miss Miller had a tight grip on the curls of her opponent.

"Tart?! I am not the one trying to trap him! I heard just now in my father's shop that you are with child. You are the one trying to force a marriage. He is mine!" Miss Smith's fist once again made contact with the face of the trollop who had seduced her dear George, just before she felt herself being pulled away.

"Let me go! I am going to make sure she never trifles with another man as long as she lives! Strumpet!"

The pair struggled against the arms that held them, each trying to get to the other to deliver more blows.

"Enough," roared Mr. Smith at the same time that Mr. Miller loudly exclaimed, "Stop!"

The two tradesmen pulled their struggling daughters back towards their respective shops, and could be heard by the gathered crowd to admonish them. "What are you thinking, airing our dirty laundry in such a way?" and "Are you daft! We could have hid your shame. Now the whole town knows!" reached across the street where the Bennet sisters stood spellbound.

Longbourn, Hertfordshire
Early March

The smell of lilacs filled the air around Elizabeth as she strolled through the gardens around her father's estate. It had been a long winter, and she was glad to be out of the house for a while. It was still too dirty to ramble beyond the hedgerows, but she could not bear to remain inside when the sun shone as it did today.

Elizabeth was fond of flowers in general, and purple lilacs in particular. They symbolized spring and the first emotions of love, both of which were very much on her mind. They were out rather early this year, too, which led her to believe her favorite of seasons was just around the corner.

This past winter had, indeed, been a long one. Her elder sister, Jane, had spent the cold months in London with their aunt and uncle. Jane had hoped to further her friendship with the sisters of the man to whom she had given her heart, a Mr. Charles Bingley. Unfortunately, the younger of his sisters, Miss Caroline Bingley, and the older, Mrs. Hurst, made it clear that the friendship was at an end. Jane never saw Mr. Bingley. Her heart was broken.

Jane's melancholy was known to the entire family. However, no one knew that Elizabeth was also nursing a bruised and battered heart.

When Mr. Bingley entered the neighborhood last autumn, he brought not only his family, but also his best friend, Mr. Darcy of Pemberley in Derbyshire. Mr. Darcy was the handsomest man she had ever seen. His dignified stance set off dark features that she could not pull her eyes away from easily. There was something about him that drew her.

Then, as she sat out a set of dances at the local assembly, she overheard him declare to his friend that she was "tolerable but not handsome enough to tempt me." The words pierced deeply into her heart. In her usual manner, she tried to turn it into a joke with those closest to her, but the barb wounded her.

That injury had made her susceptible to the charms of Mr. Wickham, the very same militia officer who, she later learned, was the cause of the scuffle in the streets of Meryton that had been talked about in the sitting rooms of the area for many weeks. Mr. Wickham was charming and filled her head with stories of Mr. Darcy and denied legacies, including a living in the church.

The day the soldier was exposed for the profligate he was shocked Elizabeth to her core. She had always thought herself to be a good judge of character, but now she knew this to, instead, be quite the flaw. Wickham made promises of marriage to several local girls, and the fight she and her sisters had witnessed had brought his schemes to light.

The scandal was the biggest to hit Meryton in years. Not only was Mr. Wickham's name bandied about, but several other officers soon found themselves accused of shameful behavior, as well. Their reputation ruined, the militia members found their welcome cut short, causing the colonel of the regiment to plead with his superiors for the authorization to make a hasty and early withdrawal of his men to their summer quarters in Brighton.

In addition, several families in the area found themselves with a daughter sent away. Thankfully, the Bennets were not counted among them. Rumor had it that Mr. Wickham received a lashing and was transferred to another unit. The entire town and not a few members of the militia breathed a sigh of relief the day the regiment marched out of Meryton.

For Elizabeth, Wickham's disgrace opened her eyes to the fact that a charming man was not necessarily a good one, and that pleasing manners did not a gentleman make. She began to look back on her interactions with Mr. Darcy with new eyes. No, he was not pleasant in company. He appeared haughty, holding himself above the neighborhood. But in close company, such as at his friend's house, he was capable of being very kind. She had, since the Assembly when his verbal barb wounded her, thought he looked at her to find fault. However, she now realized that she was the only one outside his party that he danced with at Mr. Bingley's ball. He had asked her to dance twice previous to that, as well, and she had turned him down flat both times. She began to see that perhaps in his quiet, reserved way, Mr. Darcy had been expressing admiration for her.

And so, Elizabeth's original feelings of esteem for the young man came roaring back. She knew, though, of his original opinion of her. She also knew that with Mr. Bingley gone from the neighborhood, likely at the behest of his sisters, the chances of Mr. Darcy ever returning were slim. Even if he had admired her, he could not return to Netherfield without his friend.

And really, what did she have to offer him but a thousand pounds upon her mother's death and incredibly silly relatives? No, Mr. Darcy would find and fall in love with someone who brought him far more than Elizabeth could provide. Hence, her silently bruised and battered heart.

Still, down deep inside she wished they could meet again. She would behave differently if given the opportunity; she would let him know, as much as she could within the bounds of propriety, that she had come to admire him. If only it could happen! Perhaps in London, where I will break my trip to Kent, I might see him, she thought.

Then she remembered that Miss Bingley had cut Jane; there would be no visits there, which meant no opportunity to see Mr. Darcy again. There is no real hope, is there? She sighed.

Elizabeth was not formed for melancholy, and so she did her best to put it behind her and behave as cheerfully as possible. It helped that she was soon to embark on a trip to Kent to visit her friend Charlotte, for it gave her something else upon which to focus; something to look forward to.

A few months ago, Charlotte had married William Collins, who, due to the entail put upon the property, would stand to inherit Longbourn upon Mr. Bennet's death. Mr. Collins was the rector of the parish of Hunsford, and, while visiting his cousins, had made his offer of matrimony to Elizabeth first. She, feeling he was ridiculous and nonsensical, refused his proposal.

Three days after her rejection, he proposed to Charlotte, who accepted with alacrity. While Elizabeth had not initially approved of her very good friend marrying such a ridiculous man, time and distance increased her feelings of loss for Charlotte's company and decreased her feelings of repulsion towards her cousin Collins. Therefore, she was looking forward to visiting with her friend once again.

Eventually, the chill in the air lifted and Elizabeth made her way back into the house. Entering the dining room, she sat down to break her fast with her father, currently the only other member of the house downstairs.

"Good morning, Papa." She greeted him with a smile.

"Good morning, my dear," said Mr. Bennet to his favorite daughter. "How was your walk this morning?"

Elizabeth laughed softly. "Very short, as you well know. I had to stay in the garden; it was much too dirty in the lanes even for me."

Her father chuckled. "It was kind of you to save your mother's nerves this morning. Mine appreciate it."

"You are very welcome." She grinned before turning her attention to her meal.

Her father lowered the cup of tea from which he had just taken a sip. "Lizzy, before the rest of the family invades our peace, I have a question to ask you. It involves someone no longer in the neighborhood."

"Well, since there are several people no longer in the neighborhood, I am all curiosity. Please, tell me who it is you are asking about, and what your inquiry is." Elizabeth smiled as her father smirked.

"I was wondering about one of Netherfield's former residents. In light of what we have recently learned about Mr. Wickham, how do you now feel about Mr. Darcy? Does he still seem the black-hearted villain Wickham made him out to be, or do you, perhaps, feel differently at this time?"

Mr. Bennet knew his second daughter well, and recognized her sadness no matter how hard she tried to hide it. He had been contemplating the cause for weeks, and the only thing he could imagine was if Elizabeth had expressed herself strongly about something – or someone – and suddenly found herself proved wrong with no way to make amends. With further thought, he determined that the single possibility was the gentleman from Derbyshire. There was no other person or event that had caused such a strong reaction from his usually observant daughter. Of course, she did have a temper. It was one of the characteristics she inherited from her mother. Still, she was not one to vehemently express dislike about someone in quite the insistent manner that she had about Mr. Darcy.

Elizabeth blushed. "Indeed, I feel very differently about Mr. Darcy now. Once I came to realize Mr. Wickham's penchant for embellishment, I began to think that there might be more to his story. While I cannot know exactly what happened between the two, Mr. Darcy certainly had reason to not trust such a man.

"Hmph, he certainly showed how rude he can be at the Assembly by talking so of my daughter – and in her hearing, as well," he said, reaching out to pat Elizabeth's hand in consolation.

"He should never have spoken such a thing in public about anyone." She paused, looking off unseeingly towards the wall. "He was not at all sociable at the dinners and card parties in the neighborhood, and at the time I felt he was looking down on us because he did not share much of himself with us. I thought him to be like Mr. Bingley's sisters, not speaking because he thought himself above everyone else. But then he made more of an effort to converse with me when I was at Netherfield than they did, and he did ask me to dance at the ball. I now realize he is a bit like Jane, who you know rarely shares her feelings but is always proper."

Bennet nodded and took another sip of his tea.

She looked at her father again. "How can I accept Jane's reticence, especially amongst strangers, and reject Mr. Darcy's? I cannot and still be a reasonable person."

She went on to explain how she had learned her lesson about trusting those who only appeared good rather than those who, over time, proved that they were good.

"So, you approve of Mr. Darcy now?"

Elizabeth hesitated for a moment. Her father liked to tease, but she always felt she could share everything with him. She was reluctant to reveal her secret thoughts, but knew they would not leave this room. She decided to trust him. "I do, very much. I should like an opportunity to make his acquaintance again, though I doubt I will."

"Hmm," he replied thoughtfully. Appearing to come to a decision, he rose to leave the dining room and said, "I believe, Daughter, that he liked you, as well. I would not be averse to such a man asking for your hand at some point in the future, were you to meet with him again, and if the two of you formed an attachment. It would be a comfort knowing you cared about your husband and were respected in turn."

With that, he left his greatly astonished second daughter anticipating the chaos of breakfast with her sisters and vanished into his book room.

Chapter 2

Gracechurch Street, London
Mid-March

Elizabeth was to travel first to London, where she and her companions would stay with her aunt and uncle Gardiner for a night, then on to Kent. Sir William Lucas was eager to see his eldest daughter, Charlotte, well situated with her new husband. His younger daughter, Miss Maria Lucas, was to stay with the Collinses as well, and Sir William would return home after just a week.

They arrived at Gracechurch Street, where Elizabeth's aunt and uncle and their children, as well as her dear sister Jane, were on hand to greet the party. After having some tea and some refreshments, the adults went out to do some shopping as a way to pass the day. Later they would be going to the theater.

That evening, as the group made their way into one of London's most popular playhouses, they came face to face with the one person they had least expected to see – Charles Bingley. Mr. Bingley and Mr. Darcy had been standing to one side of the lobby with Mr. Hurst, waiting for Miss Bingley and Mrs. Hurst. While Mr. Gardiner went to the window to purchase their tickets, the rest of his party moved to the same side of the lobby in order to keep open the path to the door. Jane bumped into a gentleman, gently apologizing, when the man turned around with a gasp.

"Miss Bennet!"

"Mr. Bingley!"

The two spoke at the same time, blushes covering their faces.

"How are you?" asked Mr. Bingley.

"I am well, sir," she responded softly. "May I introduce you and your party to the rest of mine?"

Seeing his nod, she began. "Sir William Lucas you know, of course, and his daughter, Miss Lucas."

Bingley bowed to them both with a delighted smile on his face. "Indeed! It is so good to see you!"

Smiling, Jane continued. "My aunt, Mrs. Edward Gardiner. I have been staying with her and my uncle since January. Mr. Gardiner is at the ticket window."

At this, Bingley startled but quickly recovered himself, declaring that he was pleased to make her aunt's acquaintance.

Finally, Miss Bennet said as she gestured to Elizabeth, "My sister you also know, of course."

Bingley smiled at her, stating, "Yes, I do. How have you been, Miss Elizabeth? It has been so long since I have seen my Hertfordshire friends. Why, it has been more than three months! Not since the twenty-sixth of November, when we were all dancing together at Netherfield!"

"You are correct, sir." Elizabeth smiled, then looked pointedly at her sister.

Bingley performed introductions for his party before turning to his friend and asking, "I say, Darcy, is there not room enough for Miss Bennet's party to join us in your box? Surely we can all squeeze quite comfortably together. What say you? And you, Mrs. Gardiner?"

Darcy jumped a little at being addressed, as his attention was entirely on Elizabeth. "Yes, we can; what an excellent idea, Bingley!"

Being behind his friend, Darcy had

been able to observe the onset of the encounter, including the look of absolute joy on Miss Bennet's face and the quick change of her expression to one of sorrow. He was astounded. Miss Bingley had assured him that Miss Bennet had no feelings for her brother, but from what he had just seen, she most certainly did. Combined with the observations he had made of his friend this past week, he was certain he had made a grave error in any advice that separated the two.

All thoughts of Bingley and Miss Bennet flew out of his head, though, the second he realized that beside Miss Bennet was the witty and vivacious Miss Elizabeth. Darcy was awestruck with the beautiful vision she presented in a light purple gown that fit her like a glove. He surreptitiously examined her figure, his eye drawn to the perfectly colored lilac blossoms woven into her hair, before looking into her eyes. What he saw there both astonished and excited him, giving him hope that had previously not existed.

Is that what I see when she looks at me? he thought. Could it truly be admiration? Darcy was overwhelmed, both by her presence and the emotion he saw. He had left Hertfordshire for two main reasons: because he admired her, and because he felt she was not an acceptable choice for his wife. There were other reasons, of course. For one thing she had defended his greatest enemy, George Wickham, with vigor. He was unsure of her feelings for the blackguard. It pained him to think she thought more highly of his adversary than she did of himself, because it did appear she did not think well of him last fall. She had brought up her new acquaintance with the other man during their one dance together, defending him most vigorously and probing insistently into

Darcy's own character. She had said things that made him think she believed whatever story Wickham told, and that she held Darcy responsible for the man's situation.

In truth, she had no reason to think well of him then. His behavior, he had come to realize, was less than gentlemanly. In the quiet of his sitting room, as he relaxed before bed, he remembered his time in Meryton and was able to examine his actions in retrospect. He recalled the things he said to Miss Bingley when he first met Elizabeth, about her not being a beauty. He implied to his friends that he thought less of her for walking three miles along dirty lanes and fields to tend to her ill sister. He sat with her for thirty minutes, never speaking a word, on her last day at Netherfield, because he was afraid of raising her expectations. Worst of all, upon the occasion of his first opportunity to be introduced to her, he insulted her within her hearing. That embarrassed him the most. He had been raised to behave better than that. Weeks of reflection showed him he did not deserve her good opinion, because he gave offense to her at every turn.

Despite this knowledge, the intervening time had only increased his feelings toward her. Seeing the look she gave him tonight, and knowing her generous nature, he began to hope her opinion of him had changed. Realizing that all along he had wanted a courtship with this wonderful woman, he had begun to question his reasons for not asking for one.

Her family's behavior was definitely not that of refined society. Her younger sisters and mother were loud, brash, and unchecked. Her father was indolent, mocking, and sarcastic. He would rather sit along the wall at the Netherfield ball and laugh at his daughters' behaviors than take the trouble to correct them, and when he did finally make an effort with his middle daughter, it was very badly done. However, if Elizabeth were to accept him, he would be marrying her, not her relations. The knowledge that Pemberley was days away from Longbourn, and visits from the Bennets to the Darcy estate would be few and far between, negated even more of that argument.

Another problem was her dowry, which was very little. However, Darcy was a wealthy man. In the five years since his father's passing, he had greatly increased his yearly income. Unlike his father and others of that generation, Darcy saw the future in the boundless proliferation of manufacturing and machines, and had chosen to invest in carefully scrutinized inventions and businesses. Every quarter saw an increase. With his income, and the potential for exponentially more, lack of a dowry was no stumbling block to a union with Miss Elizabeth.

Then, there was the lady herself. Besides her appeal physically, she was intelligent. She was well-read and not afraid to argue her position on any number of issues. She challenged him, which no other woman of his acquaintance had ever done that he could recall. She never fawned over him. He was doubly glad of this, for he hated that above all else. She was always graceful and polite; even when Miss Bingley insulted her, Miss Elizabeth answered with grace and forbearance. She could play the pianoforte and sing, and he had watched as she expertly embroidered handkerchiefs and other items. Her manners and accomplishments were not lacking. She would be an excellent wife in all ways.

All these thoughts flew through Darcy's head as he bowed and greeted each member of her party. He was surprised to learn the fashionable couple accompanying the Misses Bennet – Mr. Gardiner had rejoined his party in the middle of Bingley's introductions to his sisters – was their relatives from Gracechurch Street. He had not thought poorly about tradesmen in general, although while at Netherfield, Miss Bingley attempted to keep the party entertained with speculation about this pair in particular. Darcy was happy to see they were graceful, elegant people. From the conversation he was witnessing, they also seemed to be well-informed. Certainly there was nothing to be ashamed of there. This felt to him like another nail in the coffin of his arguments against a union with the most fascinating lady he had ever met.

Chapter 3

While Darcy was greeting her party and ruminating on her, Elizabeth's thoughts were equally full of him. She had forgotten how tall he was, and how handsome. He was very solemn as he greeted the party, yet his eyes almost caressed her, softening just the smallest bit when he looked upon her. He was gracious in his greeting to her aunt and uncle. That was a relief, though as she thought on it, Mr. Bingley's fortune was made in trade and the two were good friends. She had no real reason to think he would not have been kind and welcoming other than what Miss Bingley said many months ago. But was it truly fair to judge him by the same standard when he was not the person to espouse such notions? He was even kind to Sir William, and she knew that man sorely tried Mr. Darcy's nerves.

Elizabeth's heart beat faster than

normal to be so near to him. Still, she must not let herself get carried away. He likely never saw her as more than an acquaintance, and she knew now that he was not the monster Mr. Wickham made him out to be. She also recognized he had singled her out as a dance partner, and yet there were still the harsh words he had said the first time they met that she was not handsome. She had no reason to suppose he had changed his opinion. She must guard her heart, but oh, how she wished she did not have to do so! She turned her attention back to the conversation that continued around her.

"Mr. Bingley," Jane began, having made a decision just moments before to speak with him. "Did your intended not come with you?" She wanted to hear from his own lips about Miss Darcy so she could put her heartache behind her and move on with her life. This sort of behavior was entirely too bold for her, usually, but desperate times called for desperate measures.

Bingley looked confused, and his next words betrayed that feeling. "My intended? I am not engaged. I am not even courting anyone. Why would you think I was?"

"Oh, I am sorry, sir. In her letter, Miss Bingley seemed quite certain you and Miss Darcy would soon announce an understanding." Jane's heart was beating so fast she was sure everyone could hear it.

"My sister told you this?" Bingley looked at Hurst, who rolled his eyes and shook his head. "Why am I not surprised? My sister was wrong, Miss Bennet. Miss Darcy is not yet sixteen, and has not even had her coming out. She is much too young for me. My eye is drawn to a more mature woman to court, if she will have me."

Jane saw Bingley's intense look and

blushed. "I am sure all you need do is ask, and she would accept you."

"I certainly hope so, Miss Bennet. May I escort you to Darcy's box?" Holding out his arm to Jane, he saw his sister join them with a look of dismay on her face. His glare told her that he had something to discuss with her later.

Caroline Bingley was not happy to see the Bennets cozying up to her brother and Mr. Darcy. She could tell by the look on Charles' face that one of them related something to him that she had said. She mentally squirmed. He did control her dowry and her pin money, and he had been known in the past to curtail her spending when he did not like her behavior. He was much like their father that way. She was not looking forward to the conversation they would have later. However, she had been able to persuade him to her way of thinking in the past, so perhaps she could this time, as well.

Caroline turned to Mr. Darcy, expecting him to offer his arm to escort her as they made their way to his box. She was surprised to see he had already offered it to Elizabeth. Caroline was furious. She hated Eliza Bennet, because Eliza took Mr. Darcy's attention away from her. How was she to become Mrs. Darcy when other ladies drew him away? She examined Elizabeth with a critical eye. Her gown, while it fit well, was at least a year out of style. The lilac color was not one Caroline favored, and so she wrinkled her nose at it. Really, she thought, the girl has no taste. Then there were those ridiculous flowers in her hair. Did she not know that feathers were in style? What kind of blooms were they, anyway? She sniffed, raising her nose as she put her hand on Hurst's other arm and began walking toward the stairs.

As the party began ascending to the

floor above, Darcy leaned down to the lady on his arm. "Miss Elizabeth, how have you been?"

She smiled up at him. "Well, sir. Yourself?"

"I have been well for the most part. Only a little lonely."

She looked at him with her brows raised in surprise. "Lonely? How is that possible?"

Darcy turned that intense look upon her once more. "Yes, lonely. I have missed the company of a certain charming young lady who likes to challenge me at every turn."

Elizabeth's heart stopped for a moment before thumping loudly once again. She swallowed, almost afraid to hear the response to her question. "And, who would this charming young lady be?"

She had not thought it possible, but

his eyes became even more intense as he answered her. "You, Miss Elizabeth." He paused as she gasped. "How long will you be in town? I should like to call on you, if I may."

"Oh, Mr. Darcy, I would like that very much, but we are to leave in the morning for Kent. We are visiting my friend Charlotte and her new husband, my cousin Mr. Collins, for a few weeks."

Darcy's disappointment was clear. However, all was not lost. As he recalled, her cousin Collins was rector for his aunt, Lady Catherine. As Easter was coming soon, he would be going to Kent himself before long. They could spend time together there, and perhaps leave as an engaged couple.

"Miss Elizabeth …" He spoke quickly, as they were approaching his box and opportunity for private conversation would soon be limited. "I had thought to wait to ask you this, but in light of your trip tomorrow, I will ask now. Would you agree to a courtship with me? I know it is unusual to do so after so short an acquaintance as ours, but with you leaving in the morning, I will have no opportunity to call on you while you are here with your family. I will be in Kent soon, as well, visiting my aunt, and if we are courting it will be easier for us to spend time together. I have for months thought of you as the handsomest woman of my acquaintance, and I very much admire your spirit and intelligence. I should like us to get to know each other better; I assure you that my intentions are honorable."

Elizabeth was so astonished – shocked even – and delighted, that at first she could not think. This was a dream come true! Her eyes filled up with tears that she prayed would not overflow. "Yes, Mr. Darcy; I would like that very much. Thank you." Her response was heartfelt.

For Darcy, seeing the shock and joy in her eyes was the answer to his every hope to this point. Her happiness was plain to see, and he responded by allowing her to see his own. "Thank you, Miss Elizabeth. You have made me a very happy man." He squeezed her hand as he entered the box. He helped her to sit, then quietly asked Mr. Gardiner for a word in the hall.

When the two men came back in, her uncle squeezed Elizabeth's shoulder before moving to sit next to his wife. Mrs. Gardiner looked at him, a question in her eyes, and he leaned over to whisper the news to her.

Darcy took the seat beside Elizabeth. He leaned close and whispered, "Your uncle gave his permission, but I still must ask your father. I am due to come to Rosings in two weeks. We can court there, but it must be done quietly, as my aunt will be opposed. She has wanted me to marry my cousin for years, but neither Anne nor I have desired it."

Elizabeth nodded. From what she had gathered from her cousin of Lady Catherine's personality, she was not surprised that Darcy was hesitant to openly call on her in a place where his aunt had so much influence.

"You are aware of my fondness for walks?" She watched Darcy nod. "Are there places at Hunsford where I may continue that practice?"

Darcy grinned at her. Of course, his wise and wonderful Elizabeth would think of a perfect way to spend time together without his overbearing aunt knowing. "Indeed, there are. We could meet on one of the paths in the mornings, and I will visit as often as I can at the parsonage."

Elizabeth smiled back as the play began. She wished she could share her joy with the entire theater, but without her father's sanction of the courtship, that was not yet possible. She did her best to focus on the actors on the stage. Her hands were on the bench on either side of her, under the edges of her skirt. Soon, however, she felt her right hand covered by the large warm one of the man beside her as Darcy moved his over hers. She turned hers over and their palms clasped together. They stayed that way the entire evening, each silently enjoying the contact. Frequently, their eyes strayed from the production to each other.

Just before the end, Elizabeth covertly pulled some of the lilacs out of her hair and pressed them into his hand. His eyes thanked her as he carefully put them in his waistcoat pocket. He knew flowers had meanings, but was not familiar with the particulars of this one. He planned to remedy that deficiency in his education that night, before he went to bed. Soon, he would go to visit Mr. Bennet and gain his permission. The next two weeks could not go by fast enough to suit Mr. Darcy!

~~~***~~~

Later, after preparing for sleep, Darcy made a trip to his library to look for a book that would tell him the meanings of flowers. While not as extensive as the one at Pemberley, the library at Darcy House was large, filled with books on almost any topic one could want. Consulting the catalog his father had commissioned, Darcy made note of two or three volumes that might contain the information he needed. Pulling the first one off the shelf, he quickly leafed through it, finding, to his delight, that it was exactly the book he required. Sitting down on a sofa with the book in hand, Darcy read with joy
~~~

the meaning behind lilacs.

Purple lilacs stand for the first emotions of love, he thought, grinning. She loves me!

Darcy did not know how he was to sleep tonight with this new insight. The knowledge that Elizabeth shared his affection left him too full of excitement. He was free now to indulge and express his own sentiments. His future appeared brighter than it had before. It seemed as though all of his dreams since his time at Netherfield were coming true.

~~~***~~~

Few of the residents of the Bingley townhouse a few streets over expected to sleep anytime soon. No sooner had the family arrived home than Mr. Bingley, who had remained
~~~

silent the entire ride home from the theater, with his eyes fixed on the darkness of the window, had demanded a family conference in the drawing room. Once there, he made it clear to his sisters that he was aware of the deceptions played upon him and Miss Bennet. Caroline and Louisa stammered and sputtered, trying to explain themselves, but he was having none of it.

"What were you thinking?" Bingley paced angrily in front of the sofa on which his siblings sat. "Not only did you lie to me, you lied to one of the sweetest ladies I have ever met! She offered you her friendship, asking nothing in return, and you lied to her and cut off the relationship. You have treated her abominably! If I had not spoken to her this evening, and did not know without a shadow of a doubt that she cares for me, I would be afraid that she would not have me.

Why did you do it?" Bingley stopped and glared at them while he awaited their explanation.

Caroline spoke up. "We saved you from an imprudent connection. I fail to see what the problem here is. She is beneath you …"

"Enough!" roared Bingley, his countenance red. "In case you had not noticed before, she is a gentleman's daughter. You are not, nor am I a gentleman's son. Marriage to her would be a step up for me."

Louisa spoke next. "But her family …"

"Are wonderful people. They are exuberant, yes, but I would not be marrying her family. And before you say anything else …" He held up his hand as Caroline and Louisa opened their mouths. "I do intend to marry her if she will have me. I am angrier with you about your treatment of Miss Bennet than your treatment of your own brother, but I am also hurt that you would use deception to separate me from someone I love. Sisters who cared would not do such a thing."

At this, they had the grace to look away in shame, though that did not stop them from trying again.

"Really, Charles …" began Caroline just as Louisa started to say, "But …"

At this point, Mr. Hurst intervened. "That will be all, Louisa." He stood up to look at his gaping wife, who was not used to her husband saying much of anything to her that was not related to his meals, his sport, or his port. "I have not the authority to stop Caroline, but I do over you. It was wrong of you to lie, and you know it. The time has come for you to discontinue allowing your sister to sway you into doing and saying things you should not. Or, perhaps more accurately, it is time I stopped permitting you. You will apologize to your brother and to Miss Bennet the next time you see her. Do you understand?"

Louisa nodded. While she was not sure she liked being spoken to in that manner, she felt a stirring of something inside at the sound of his tone of voice. He had never before been so firm with her; he had always permitted her to follow her sister and had never made demands on her. She had spent most of their marriage wishing he was not so weak. Now, however, something in him seemed to have suddenly changed. He had spoken to her with a tone of command that she felt herself responding to. Perhaps allowing him to exert his role as head of their household, as the husbands of her friends did in theirs, might be a good thing. She was willing to find out, she decided, and when he beckoned her to join him to go up to their rooms, she quickly rose to comply.

Caroline watched this transpire with a cynical twist to her lips. She did not understand her sister's easy compliance with her worthless husband. She would certainly never let Mr. Darcy treat her in such a way once they married. Her still-enraged brother interrupted her thoughts.

"Caroline, I am done with you – with both of you. That you would betray me is inconceivable, and yet, you have. Words cannot convey the depth of my anger. I will be moving out. You will stay here with the Hursts. I expect you to marry this season, and I do not mean to Darcy. You will attend every ball and dinner you are invited to and you will be encouraging to possible suitors. You will hopefully get an offer of marriage, and you will accept it. I do not care who he is or from what level of society. If you do not marry this season, I will set you up with your own establishment and you will live alone." Once again, Bingley was pacing angrily back and forth in front of her, speaking in an uncharacteristically loud voice. Raising his hand and pointing toward the door, he finished with, "I am done with you. Go to bed; get out of my sight before I say something I will truly regret."

Having never seen him in such a state, his sister decided to try to talk sense into him another day. Silently she rose and did as he bid.

Chapter 4

For Elizabeth, the two weeks she waited for Darcy at Hunsford were very long. She spent the first few days getting reacquainted with her friend and resting from the journey. She was very happy that Charlotte appeared content with her new situation. While Elizabeth certainly would not have been able to abide marriage to her cousin, it appeared that her friend had the ability to manage him quite well. She was never disrespectful of him, and she had all the appearance of listening to and agreeing with his every word. However, she somehow always seemed to get things done her own way. Elizabeth rather admired Charlotte's ability to administer her household.

So far, the Hunsford party had been to Rosings to dine twice during the first fortnight of her visit, and had been invited to take tea an additional three times. At each meeting, Lady Catherine had interrogated her rector's cousin on her family and upbringing. Her questions had been intrusive and repetitive – to the point that Elizabeth was ready to scream. However, she was a gentlewoman, and was not about to return rudeness for rudeness. She did, use her wit to quiet the lady once or twice, though. That was far more satisfying than acting in a way that would show her own manners to be lacking.

Elizabeth spent much of her time in the mornings walking the gardens of the manor. Unerringly, she found the lilac bushes she loved so much in full bloom. She spent hours amongst them, sometimes sitting on the stone bench placed there, reading or daydreaming of Mr. Darcy. Other times found her wandering around them while thoughts of him filled her mind. She wondered if he knew what lilacs stand for in the language of flowers.

She turned and he was there, walking towards her, a large bunch of the fragrant purple flowers in his left hand, his right hand moving up to remove his hat. He stopped as he bowed to her, then stretched the flowers out for her to take. "For you," he whispered. As she took the bouquet into her own hands, his slid up her arm to her elbow and he leaned towards her, eyes on her lips. "You are so beautiful," he breathed just before his mouth captured hers in a breathtaking kiss.

Elizabeth sighed. Soon, she hoped, her daydreams would become reality.

Often, she would work with Charlotte in the still room, turning flower petals from the parsonage's garden into perfumes and lotions. This was something she enjoyed and did well, especially when she shared the task with a friend. The two ladies spent many pleasurable hours working together.

On mornings when she wanted a change, or perhaps had some extra time to fill, Elizabeth wandered the paths in the groves. Rosings had many kinds of trees, some that would bear nuts and fruits, and others just nice to look at, all providing shade from the sun and protection from the elements. Many of these paths seemed to be traversed rarely, and would be wonderful places to visit with her suitor. She looked forward to his arrival.

~~~***~~~

For Darcy, the two weeks also progressed slowly. He had settled some business with his attorney, inspected the mistress' chambers at
~~~

Darcy House, noting some changes to discuss with the housekeeper, and spent time with his sister. He attended a couple family dinners, but refused to attend balls when his aunt tried to insist. He had neither reason nor desire to attend, as he was no longer looking for a wife.

He could not tell his aunt this, of course. Lady Matlock had definite standards about potential wives, and Elizabeth did not meet those ideals. No, what she had was worth far more to Darcy than anything his aunt might require. He also had to consider that he had not yet spoken to Mr. Bennet. No one could be told anything until he had that gentleman's permission.

Darcy waited a week before visiting Longbourn. Elizabeth had asked him to give her time to warn her father of his coming, and had written a letter to be posted the day she left for Kent. Darcy was of two minds about this. On one hand, he was glad the gentleman was not going to be surprised, for it would make the visit less awkward. On the other hand, the delay gave him more time to think, which made him more nervous. To combat his nerves, he planned out and repeatedly rehearsed his speech. This gave him the confidence to proceed, knowing he was less likely to stumble over his tongue and say the wrong thing.

On the day of the visit, Darcy set out on horseback at an early hour. The ride was pleasant, as the weather was fine. He stopped a few times to take refreshment, and arrived at Longbourn about mid-day. He knocked on the door and was admitted by the housekeeper. Was her name Hill or Mill? He could not recall which it was. He handed her his card and asked to speak to Mr. Bennet. He hoped his presence remained unknown to Mrs. Bennet to prevent inciting her nerves.

Soon he was following Hill to Mr. Bennet's book room, where he was announced and given admittance.

"Mr. Darcy, welcome! Fine morning for an extended ride, is it not?" Bennet bowed, greeting the man who had apparently gained his Lizzy's approbation. "Please, sit."

Darcy bowed, as well. "Thank you, sir," he said as he settled into a chair. "It was indeed a fine morning for a ride. You are well, I hope? And your family?"

"We are well, thank you. I understand from Lizzy that you have seen her and Jane in town recently?" He leaned back in his chair as he spoke, elbows on the arms and fingers interlocked over his belly.

"Yes, sir, I have. We saw each other at the theater about a week ago, the night before she left for Kent. She and Miss Bennet were attending a play and we chanced upon each other in the lobby." Darcy sat stiffly upright, hands clasped in his lap.

"Indeed. It seems from my daughter's letter that you have asked for a courtship? And she has consented?"

"Yes, sir. I am here to ask for your permission to court Miss Elizabeth. I am hoping the courtship leads to marriage. I feel we are well-suited to each other, and once we get to know each other better, I intend to make her an offer. She is in agreement; all we need to proceed is your consent."

Mr. Bennet smiled. "Well, Mr. Darcy, you have it. Lizzy and I spoke of you in the aftermath of Mr. Wickham's downfall, so I already knew that her opinion of you had softened. I have suspected for some time that she might be feeling regret at your leaving."

"Thank you, sir." Darcy let out a

relieved breath. He had not realized until just now how tightly he had been holding himself. A brilliant smile lit his face. Suddenly, he startled.

"Mr. Wickham, sir? What did that scoundrel do now? I should have made his character known before I left the area. Let me apologize now for my lack of diligence. Please, sir, tell me he did no harm to your family?"

Impressed with this speech, Bennet replied, "No, he did not harm my family. He did, however, injure a few of the daughters of the area. Two of them had a physical altercation in the street, which let the cat out of the bag, so to speak. It was not long before the man's debaucheries were public knowledge, trumpeted all over Hertfordshire. It is my understanding that he was flogged and sent to another regiment." He shook his head. "Of course, he had more sins to his name than just those with young ladies. He had debts to the very same tradesmen whose daughters he had meddled with, in addition to gambling debts amongst his fellow officers. I know not where he was sent, nor do I care. I am simply glad that none of my children are spending the rest of their lives in a far off county raising illegitimate children."

He paused and offered his guest a glass of port. "I will be forever grateful, though, that my eyes have been opened to the dangers of unattached young men. I can see by the look in your eye that you recognize my passivity in raising my children and do not agree with it. I have been lazy, I admit, and I fight daily with myself to change, but I am more aware now of what my girls are doing and with whom. Officers have been banned from the house. They will always be silly, my daughters, but I can protect them, and I will."

Darcy accepted the wine, saying, "That is good to hear, sir. It is an unfortunate fact that many men of all levels of society view young ladies as prey to be vanquished, with no thought to their futures or reputations. Mr. Wickham has pleasant manners, and to one unfamiliar with him, he would seem an honest and upright person. But his personality is base and his proclivities equally so. Nothing would have stopped him from making a conquest, and he cares for none but himself. The area is well rid of him."

Bennet was intrigued by his guest's passionate response. "It seems, sir, that you have been more than once affected by this snake?"

"Yes, sir. He was the son of my father's steward; my father was his godfather. We were raised together." Darcy's voice became softer as he remembered his childhood companion. "His viciousness could be seen at an early age if one cared to look, and by the time we were at school together and out from under our fathers' eyes, Wickham had become very wild. Cards and women took more of his time than lectures and study. I took care that my father did not know; I paid Wickham's debts and paid off his women many times out of my allowance."

Darcy paused to take a sip of his port. Bennet waited patiently, as he knew there was more to the story than what had been reported so far.

"When my father died, he left godson one thousand pounds and a valuable living, provided he took orders. Wickham declared his intention to study the law instead, and accepted three thousand pounds in lieu of the living. He signed a document resigning his rights to it. I was sure I had heard the last of him, but when the rector passed away, Wickham was back with his hand out, demanding his inheritance. I refused, of course, and that is when he began spreading his vitriol about me." Here he paused, gathering his thoughts and emotions. "I thought he was gone from my life after that, until last summer, when he tried to convince my sister to elope. If I had not come to visit unexpectedly, she may have been lost forever. As it is, she was left heartbroken; she was just fifteen."

Bennet let out a breath that he had been unaware he was holding. "Well, Mr. Darcy, considering it had been mere weeks since you experienced that unhappy event, you certainly had reason to be unpleasant when you arrived at that first assembly. I am happy you saved your sister; please know that what you have told me will not leave this room."

Rising, Darcy thanked him. "I leave for Rosings in another day or two. Do you have any messages for Miss Elizabeth? I would be glad to pass them on for you."

"I will send her a letter, express, telling her that I granted permission. Receiving an express ought to give her and my cousin's household a bit of excitement for a few days." He chuckled at the thought.

"Oh, I nearly forgot. My aunt, Lady Catherine, has been declaring my engagement to her daughter since I was young. My father specifically told me I was only to marry her if she was truly my choice, and that I was not to allow Lady Catherine to push me to do something I was unwilling to do. Miss Elizabeth is aware of this, and she agrees that we must court quietly until we can both leave the area." Darcy flushed a deep red. "I do not trust my aunt to behave as she should. She is a scheming woman, and overbearing, and will attempt to make trouble for us. We will wait to announce our courtship until one or both of us are ready to leave Kent. Please be aware, sir; I fear she is capable of anything."

"I will keep that in mind." Mr. Bennet was growing concerned. "Are there others of your family who might cause trouble?"

"No, sir. My aunt is not the only one who imagines she can control me, but she is the only one who does not give way when I refuse to cooperate. The rest of my family may rail at me a bit, but they are aware that I am my own man. They will not cause trouble."

Bennet briefly closed his eyes. Then, exhaling quietly, he replied. "That is good to know. I will watch for anything untoward from Kent, then. Thank you for the warning."

"Mr. Bennet." Darcy paused, unsure if he should go on. "Sir, if while we are at Rosings, I feel the time is right to propose, do I have your permission to do so? Do I have your permission to marry your daughter?" He was uncertain why he felt it so important to ask this question now; some unseen force propelled him and he was helpless to do aught but follow.

His companion laughed. "Yes, Mr. Darcy, if your courtship progresses in Kent to the point that you feel it is time to propose, you have my permission to marry Lizzy. Just make sure the proprieties are kept. No elopements."

"You may be sure of my cooperation on that account."

With that, the two men shook hands, and, bowing, Darcy took his leave to begin his journey back to London. He was grateful for Bennet's permission to court Elizabeth, for the chance to explain himself, and for the knowledge that Wickham had, for once in his life, been punished for his misdeeds.

Chapter 5

The day finally came that would see Darcy arrive at Rosings. Knowing that, for now, the residents of the manor and the parsonage must remain unaware of their courtship, Elizabeth did not expect to see him for another day or two. Her surprise and delight was great indeed when, on the day after his arrival, he and his cousin, Colonel Fitzwilliam, walked to the rectory to visit. They had accompanied Mr. Collins, who had gone up to Rosings to pay his respects.

Charlotte saw them coming, and said to Elizabeth, not knowing how true her words were, "We have you to thank for this, Eliza. Mr. Darcy would not have called upon me so promptly were you not here." Elizabeth blushed, but said nothing.

When the men entered and greetings had been exchanged, everyone took a seat and Charlotte prepared to pour tea. Elizabeth had chosen to sit on the settee, and Darcy joined her there, enabling him to speak quietly to her with more ease. Waiting until the rest of the room was engaged in listening to a story the colonel was telling, Darcy leaned over towards Elizabeth and whispered, "Your father has given his permission for us to court. He said he would write to you?"

Elizabeth nodded. She had received the express. It was devoid of much of the teasing she expected, but she attributed that to her Papa's sure knowledge that she must keep certain information to herself, yet explain matters to the household in such a way that they understood the letter did not contain bad news. It simply stated that he had received an unexpected visitor the day before and that the results of that meeting were satisfactory to all. If Mr. Collins was overly curious, that was his problem to address, as the contents of her letters were none of his business.

"Yes, I received the news." Elizabeth smiled at him and glanced around. Seeing that the rest of the group was still listening raptly to the colonel, she continued. "I have found many beautiful paths in the area. There is an open grove along this side of the park that seems to be infrequently visited. Perhaps you might join me one morning in viewing it?"

Darcy smiled back at her in delight. "I am sure that can be arranged. When do you take your walks?"

"In the very early morning. Will you be able to rise early enough, do you think?" Her eyes twinkled as she teased him.

"I shall beat you to the grove, my dear," he whispered back.

~~~***~~~

The next morning at dawn found the pair greeting each other in the grove with wide smiles. They spent a pleasant hour or two asking questions of each other designed to uncover similarities and differences between them. They discovered they both enjoyed Shakespeare and Cowper, and Darcy liked Donne while Elizabeth preferred Wordsworth. Histories were a favorite subject shared by the pair; however, Elizabeth liked to indulge in the occasional novel where Darcy spurned them.

Subsequent mornings were spent similarly, engaging in lighthearted banter and searching inquiries, serious discussions and periods of levity. One of the more somber subjects they canvassed was that of Mr. Wickham. Elizabeth shared with Darcy her view
~~~

of the events in Meryton and how they had affected her, revealing not only Wickham's true character, but Darcy's, as well. He shared with her his initial reservations about a union with her and how he had overcome them. These two conversations caused some anger and hurt feelings on both sides, but communication, holding of hands, and a few tender hugs soothed them and they were able to move on to other topics. They each felt too much for the other to let the past come between them now that they had found each other.

Another topic they discussed was Darcy's cousin, the colonel. Elizabeth had taken note on their first visit upon arriving at Rosings that the man seemed to be trying to keep the attention of Mr. and Mrs. Collins, so that she and Darcy would be able to talk.

"What does Colonel Fitzwilliam know of us, Mr. Darcy?"

"I have told him that we are courting. He is my closest friend, after Bingley, and shares guardianship of Georgiana with me. He told me after meeting you that he thoroughly approves, not that I need his approval, of course. Though, it will help us to win his parents' approbation. He has distracted our aunt several times so that you and I could continue our morning walks unmolested, and has covered for me when I have been late returning." Darcy laughed. "He told me if he had met you first, I would not have stood a chance, and that he would have won your hand. I believe he admires you."

"Oh," Elizabeth said, turning towards him. "I would not want to come between you!"

"I was teasing, my love. He does like you, but not in a romantic sense."

Letting out a huge breath, she replied, "I am glad to hear it."

Several times over the course of the gentlemen's visit at Rosings, the parsonage residents were asked to dine at the manor, or to come for tea. These times were difficult for the quietly courting couple, as they wished to sit together and talk but could not for fear of discovery. Similarly, Darcy and the colonel walked to the parsonage several times, but the ever present threat that someone would detect their courtship took some of the pleasure out of the visits. Still, they took what satisfaction they could from the encounters knowing that one day soon they would not have to be secretive. Both longed for that day to come.

Eventually, the week they were to leave arrived. On Monday, during their walk, Darcy asked the all-important question. Elizabeth had been half-expecting it for days, and had her answer prepared. There was no question of her acceptance. She loved him. He was everything she had always wished for in a husband and none of what that lying Mr. Wickham had accused him of. He was respectful of her always, physically and intellectually. He was kind, and generous, and despite his stern demeanor, she easily discerned his sensitive soul. He had a touch of arrogance to be sure, but all he needed was a bit of liveliness to soften his rough edges, and Elizabeth was sure she could provide that in abundance.

Darcy was never more certain than he was now that Elizabeth was the woman with whom he would happily spend the rest of his life. She was a gentlewoman, with perfect comportment. That slight hint of impertinence in her manner was unlike most society ladies, but he was positive it would hold her in good stead as she carved her place among them. Her wit was second only to her looks, in his eyes. He was aware that her mother considered Jane the beauty of the Bennet family, but he disagreed. Elizabeth's sparkling eyes added something more to her features than what her sister had. Add to them the enticing smile that was almost always on her lips and she became a living, breathing goddess. She took his breath away.

Finally, she was intelligent and well-read, and enjoyed debating. He would not have to suffer a boring wife. If that was what he had wanted, he could have chosen a woman to please the countess, or married his cousin Anne. No, Elizabeth made him want to be a better man; that is what he had been searching for all this time. Now that he had found it, he was not about to let it go.

He was certain that Elizabeth felt similarly. The looks she bestowed on him made his heart race and his brain stop. Many times over the course of their courtship, he had almost been overwhelmed with the desire to kiss her in front of everyone. However, he respected her too much to risk putting her in a compromising position. He knew that their time at Rosings was short, and he wanted to leave there an engaged man. He had been practicing his proposal for days. The time had come to ask.

They had been walking in the grove in companionable silence for about a half-hour when Darcy stopped, causing Elizabeth to stop also. Turning so he was facing her, he took both of her hands in his.

"Elizabeth, when you first consented to allow my courtship, you gave me a sprig of flowers. Lilacs. When I got home that night, I searched my library until I found a book that would tell me the meaning of flowers. When I learned that purple lilacs, the very color of the blooms you gave me, symbolize the first emotions of love, I knew that you shared my feelings." He squeezed her hands, looking deeply into her eyes and rejoicing internally when she squeezed back. "Over the past few weeks, we have spent many delightful hours in this grove, learning more about each other. I have learned, Miss Elizabeth Bennet, that you are everything my heart told me you would be. You are witty, intelligent, and so very beautiful. You are everything I have looked for in a wife, and more. You challenge and entice me, and I desire above all else to experience this every day the rest of my life. Will you marry me?"

There was no hesitation in his beloved's response. If anything, she was barely able to hold herself back until he was done speaking. "Yes! Yes, I will marry you," she said fervently, with tears of joy in her eyes and a bright smile on her face.

"Thank you, my love," breathed Darcy. "I adore you."

So saying, he took her into his arms and did what he had long desired to do … he kissed her.

Chapter 6

The couple was due to leave in two days, so rather than his betrothed traveling post for even part of the journey to London, Darcy arranged with Mr. and Mrs. Collins to take Elizabeth and Miss Lucas in his carriage, along with his cousin and a maid to ensure propriety was observed. Charlotte at first thought it was odd her friend did not protest his offer, but the longer she contemplated it, the more certain she became that Elizabeth and the gentleman had come to an understanding. She would have thought Lizzy would be eager to share such news, but as her friend had said nothing, and it would not do to pry, she let it go. She would be told when she needed to know. She was confident of that fact.

When Lady Catherine was told of the new travel arrangements, she was unsure what to think – or what to say.

After some quick mental gyrations, she decided that Darcy was simply being gentlemanly. He was engaged to Anne, after all. Therefore, she was quick to praise him at dinner the night before their trip.

Having thus convinced herself, she was greatly shocked late the next morning when he told her of his engagement to the lowly Miss Bennet.

"Good morning, Nephew," she said as he joined her in the drawing room.

"Aunt," he replied, bowing his head briefly to her. "I am surprised to see you earlier than I intended to depart, but I am happy you are here, for it makes it much easier for me to relay an important piece of information to you."

Lady Catherine's brows rose. If he was intending to formalize his understanding with her daughter, this was an odd time to discuss it. She waited to see what he would say.

"I am happy to announce to you my engagement to Miss Elizabeth Bennet. I spoke to her father recently, and received his permission. Given your belief that I would marry my cousin, we thought it prudent to wait until we were ready to depart before giving you the news." It was now Darcy's turn to await a reaction from his aunt. He looked expectantly at her.

For a full minute, she was speechless, but then her brain engaged and her mouth exploded with anger and resentment.

"And what of Anne? You would shame her with a broken engagement? No! You will break off this farce of an understanding with that upstart now, and we will send notice to your solicitor to begin writing the contract for your marriage to my daughter." The lady's voice grew increasingly loud.

Darcy attempted to remain calm but

firm. This was, after all, his mother's sister, and of all members of his family, the most insistent upon having her own way. "No, Aunt. There has never been an engagement between my cousin and myself. My father specifically told me not to marry her if it was against my will. I do not love her, and she does not love me."

He held up his hand as she started to speak. "I have spoken with Anne already. Indeed, we spoke of it years ago; she does not desire to marry me any more than I want to marry her. We talked again last week and her thoughts and feelings have not changed. I will not marry where I do not wish to. I am my own man, head of the Darcy family. You are my mother's sister, but you do not rule me. I will marry Miss Bennet. All that is left for you is to decide if you will accept her or not. Your approbation guarantees your future invitations to our homes. Your disapprobation immediately bars you from them. The choice is entirely yours."

"Acceptance will never come from me," Lady Catherine spat. "You will come to rue your 'choice', as will she. I will personally see to it."

"You do not hold as much power as you think you do. I have already received permission from Mr. Bennet to court and to propose to Miss Bennet. He has been warned of your proclivities towards interference. He will not be moved from his consent. Neither will Lord and Lady Matlock resist my choice. You are well aware that as a family, we must stand together to avoid gossip and scandal. Be aware that it will not be myself or my betrothed who would suffer in such a situation. Nor will it be her family. It will be you who is derided. You are a stubborn woman, Aunt, but I am more so. You will lose. Desist now while your reputation is intact, for it will not be for long if you cause trouble for my betrothed or me. Good day."

With that, Darcy turned and left the room, Lady Catherine's invectives ringing in his ears. He had known it would not go well, this interview, so he had made arrangements ahead of time to have the carriage, and its passengers from the parsonage, ready to go at a moment's notice. This enabled him to make a quick getaway, entering the equipage almost before the groom got the door all the way open. Banging on the roof with his walking stick, he tried to calm himself in the few minutes he had before seeing Elizabeth. It would not do to upset her.

Colonel Fitzwilliam had been awaiting him inside the carriage. "Was it bad?" he asked.

Darcy sighed. "No worse than I

expected, I suppose. She is determined to have her way; I expect trouble in the near future. Have you written to your father?"

"Yes, I sent an express immediately upon hearing your news. I told him that Miss Bennet is a well-bred gentlewoman and would make a fine mistress of Pemberley. I am sure I did not allay all his fears, but I also told him you were set in your decision and reminded him that you are deliberate in everything you do. You would not choose someone who would do you no credit."

"Thank you, Fitzwilliam. Your support is very much appreciated." Darcy leaned his now-aching head back against the cushions for the short ride to the parsonage.

In a very few minutes, he was entering the Collinses' house. What he found there was an uproar every bit as upsetting as what he had just experienced with his aunt.

Elizabeth and Darcy had agreed to tell their relatives their joyous news immediately before leaving today. Elizabeth, knowing Mr. Collins as she did, had decided to tell Charlotte and ask her to tell her husband after she was gone. However, Collins, coming home unexpectedly early, had entered the room in the middle of her tale, unknown to both his wife and her friend. Overhearing her news, he had immediately taken her to task on behalf of his patroness, who had frequently indicated to them all that Mr. Darcy was already engaged to Miss de Bourgh. When his cousin had repeatedly refuted his words, insisting that she was engaged to the gentleman, and that they had her father's permission, he had become increasingly enraged. Was it not bad enough that she had spurned his own offer? How could she possibly think she was good enough for the illustrious nephew of his most esteemed patroness? She was a mercenary, thieving trollop!

It was at this point that Darcy entered the room. Already angry, when he heard the browbeating his beloved Elizabeth was receiving from the rector, he became even more enraged. Before he knew it, he was towering over the shorter man, his most intimidating scowl on his face.

"Mr. Collins," he barked, taking note of the surprise and fear in his adversary's eyes. "Who do you think you are to insult my betrothed in such a manner? I should call you out for that!"

Mr. Collins quivered in fear. He knew that dueling, though illegal, was still done. He further knew that the weapons used were either pistols or swords, neither of which he had been trained to use. He had tried shooting once as a youth, when a neighbor had offered to teach him. His training lasted one lesson, and was forever cancelled when he had accidentally shot his teacher in the leg. After that, it was decided that he was too awkward and clumsy to attempt to use a weapon, and no further instruction was offered or accepted.

His fear, however, did not preclude him from trying to convince the obviously errant nephew of the gracious and esteemed Lady Catherine to give up Elizabeth Bennet, and marry the lady he was formed for – his cousin, Miss de Bourgh. But it seemed Darcy was bent on having his own way, for every time Collins tried to speak to him to sway him in the proper direction, the man seemed to grow not only taller, but angrier.

"But, Mr. Darcy, sir! Your esteemed aunt, Lady Catherine, has plainly stated you are to marry your illustrious cousin, Miss de Bourgh! She cannot be wrong about this. She and your mother planned this union in your cradles! My cousin Elizabeth is not worthy of the Darcy name! She comes from such lowly stock; she has no connections of value – well, other than myself – to bring to you, and she is impoverished! She has thrown herself at you in a most unseemly way! She is a scheming, impertinent thing! She will do you no credit, sir! I must insist you honor …"

During his tirade, Collins either failed to notice, or simply ignored, the growing anger on Darcy's face. It was not until he suddenly found himself pressed against the back of a tall chair that he realized just what effect his words had on his patroness's nephew.

"My supposed engagement to my cousin is none of your concern, Mr. Collins," Darcy said, with a deadly hardness in his voice. "In addition, your cousin, my betrothed, Miss Elizabeth, is one of the finest ladies I have ever known. Do not speak of things you do not understand, sir! I would be well within my rights to call you out for insulting her! Is that what you desire?"

Mr. Collins swallowed and squeaked out a, "No, sir." He knew that someone with as much social standing as Mr. Darcy would likely get away with anything, and heaven knew he himself was not proficient enough with weapons of any sort to come out the winner of such a contest.

After two or three additional attempts to convince Darcy, the rector began to fear for his person, if not his life, and ceased further endeavors. He instead began to flatter the man, hoping to appease him.

Darcy was not fooled by the rector's apparent change of heart. Angrily, he said, "Go to Rosings and commiserate with my aunt, if you have a mind to as her parson, but do not say another word to, or about, Elizabeth. And if I hear you have given your wife, or even the Bennets, difficulty about this, I will be back and you will face me on the field of honor. Do you understand me, Mr. Collins?"

Gulping loudly, the man nodded repeatedly, backing away from Darcy and out the drawing room door. Colonel Fitzwilliam, who had followed his cousin into the house, stepped quickly aside so as not to be trampled upon by the almost-running clergyman.

Turning to Elizabeth, Darcy took a deep breath and claimed her hands. "Are you well, my dear? I apologize for losing my temper. I should not have done so." In truth, he was still enraged and it clearly showed in his mien.

"I am well, darling." Elizabeth pulled one of her hands out of his grasp and reached up to touch his face. "Thank you for defending me so ably, my knight in shining armor."

Darcy smiled at that. Leave it to this wonderful woman, his woman, to calm him and make him forget his anger. Oh, how he loved her!

The colonel, seeing that his cousin was losing himself in Miss Bennet's sparkling eyes, reminded Darcy of their current circumstances. "Darcy, perhaps we should hurry this along. We have no idea what Lady Catherine may be doing; we should go as far as we can, as fast as we can." He chuckled to himself at the sight of his staid cousin showing so much emotion. Never had he thought he would see such a thing.

"You are right, Richard." Darcy looked from the colonel to his betrothed.

"Why do we not farewell Mrs. Collins and get on our way, my love? I am eager to leave this place as I never have been before."

Not too long after, Elizabeth, Maria Lucas, and one of the Collinses' maids was in the carriage along with Darcy and the colonel, and they were on their way. Thankfully, everyone's trunks had already been packed and waiting by the door when the carriage arrived. While Darcy and Collins had been arguing, the coachman and footmen had been loading them up.

The horses were changed in Bromley, where the party took some refreshment, and they were in Gracechurch Street before tea, the fine weather assisting them in making it an easy trip.

The entire group was greeted enthusiastically by the elder Gardiners, the children being already ensconced in the nursery for the night. Once introductions to the colonel had been made, for he had not been in attendance at the theater the night they met Darcy, the group retired to the dining room. Darcy and Fitzwilliam were invited to stay for the meal, and gratefully accepted.

Following an excellent dinner in first-rate company, Darcy and Colonel Fitzwilliam took their leave, heading to Darcy House for some well-deserved rest. Worn out from emotion and travel, they agreed to retire to their respective chambers for the night. The colonel, being one of Darcy's closest relations as well as one of Georgiana's guardians, was permanently assigned a room, so that he did not have to travel back to his barracks, or even as far as his parents' house, late at night.

Knowing that it would be late when he and his cousin arrived home, Darcy had sent an express to his housekeeper before leaving Gracechurch Street, requesting baths for himself and the colonel. As he soaked in the warm water after more thoroughly scrubbing the road dust from his hair and body than he had been able to prior to his meal at the Gardiners', Darcy reflected on his day. He was still angry with his aunt and her pastor, but the urge to do violence had passed. However, he vowed again to make miserable the life of anyone, regardless of who they were, who gave his Elizabeth and her family grief, or who made any attempt to separate her from him.

His thoughts next turned to his beautiful betrothed. She was everything he could wish for. He wanted to do something special for her, to show her his love. He recalled that when he had researched the symbolism of flowers, he had learned that lavender stood for love and devotion. He was certainly devoted to her, and was very much in love with her. He thought for a while, finally coming to a decision. He knew that lavender was now in bloom, as he had seen some in the gardens at Rosings just recently. He would take her a bouquet made up of the flowers tomorrow. Surely shops here in town would have them.

Getting out of his bath and putting on his robe, Darcy went into his dressing room to don his nightshirt before climbing into his bed. Lying back, hands behind his head with fingers locked, he went over his plan for the next morning, mentally reviewing flower shops he knew. Finally, he gave in to the exhaustion and fell asleep, a smile on his lips.

Chapter 7

At the Gardiner home, Elizabeth had bathed and dressed in her nightclothes, and was sitting in front of the fire in the room she shared with Jane, drying her hair. She and her favorite sister were sharing everything that had happened in the weeks they had been apart.

"Oh, Lizzy, it is all so romantic! Who would have thought that the reserved Mr. Darcy would have such beautiful words inside him?"

Elizabeth laughed at the dreamy tone of Jane's voice. "To one who does not know him well, it would be quite the surprise, I am sure, but having spoken to him almost daily for a month, and learning what was in his heart, I was not at all startled. I was probably too eager to hear his words; I barely waited for him to finish proposing before I accepted."

Jane laughed along with her younger sister. "I can easily picture that!"

"Enough about me, Jane! Tell me what has happened with you. You seem so much happier than you were when I left."

With a smile and a blush, Jane looked down at her lap. "Mr. Bingley has been to call." She paused. "No, that is not entirely honest. Let me share with you from the beginning."

Taking a deep breath, she began. "The day you left, almost at tea time, Mr. Bingley came to call. He had quite a tale to tell, and it was clear that he was distressed. The night of our theater visit, when we sat in Mr. Darcy's box?" She looked up and, seeing Elizabeth's nod, continued. "That night, after we separated following the performance, Mr. Bingley took his sister into his study and asked her about me, and why she had not told him of my being in town. Eventually, after what I understand to be a spectacular argument, he gleaned from her that not only had I been here for weeks, but that I had visited their house. Oh, Lizzy, his anger, even hours after their confrontation, was frightening to behold."

Elizabeth got up and sat on the bed next to her sister, reaching for her hand. "And what was the result of this meeting?"

"He said that he did not sleep a wink that night. He was so upset that he had put his trust in her. He said, right in front of Aunt Gardiner, that he had been on the verge of proposing in Hertfordshire and was angry with himself as much as with her, for if he had not listened to her, he would be a happily married man by now. He then apologized for being so faithless and asked if he might formally court me and try to regain my good opinion. Oh, Lizzy, I was so happy!"

Elizabeth squeezed her hand. "I am happy for you! What else happened?"

"At first, I told aunt that I would have gladly accepted his hand, but she helped me to see that such an action would have been too impulsive. I must allow him to court me, and question him, and make sure we are compatible and that he can prove himself steady. He must be allowed to assure me that he will not do something like this again. Now that we are courting, I am enjoying this time. He rode to Longbourn, and received Papa's permission, of course. And since he returned to London, he has visited every day, and we have gone on outings to museums, parks, and the theater."

She paused, not sure how to relate the rest to Elizabeth. It was difficult for tender-hearted Jane to imagine doing such a thing to a sister, regardless of said sister's actions.

"He has removed himself from his family's townhouse and has been staying at Darcy House. He received permission from Mr. Darcy the day you left for Kent; Miss Darcy has gone to stay with an aunt and uncle and the house was going to be empty, so it was the perfect solution. He said he can no longer trust Miss Bingley, and while he cannot remove her from his protection, he can leave her to his other sister and her husband. He has not said as much, but I got the impression that he blames Mrs. Hurst, as well, for our separation. He insists that Caroline marry this season or he will set her up in her own establishment and release her dowry to her. She is of age, and legally, he can do this, it seems." She looked down at their entwined hands. "He says he does not want her in our house when we marry." She blushed. "And he says that he will court me for as long as it takes because he does intend to marry me."

Elizabeth laughed at this. "Well, I would hope so! How long do you intend to make him wait? I was so proud of you at the theater that night, showing him how you felt! I wanted to cheer!"

Jane smiled again as her blush deepened. "I felt very uncomfortable, but I needed to know, so I could banish him from my heart completely. I am so glad I did! Who knew it would have such a happy outcome?"

"And now, perhaps, you might hint to him to move matters further along? Would it not be the happiest thing for us to marry together?"

"A double wedding? Oh, how exciting! That is a wonderful idea, but perhaps we should ask Mr. Darcy and Mr. Bingley if they approve? It would not do to force them into something they did not want." Jane looked up at her sister quickly, then back down. "Of course, Mr. Bingley has not yet proposed. But, perhaps, hearing of his friend's happiness with you will help him along."

She looked at Elizabeth out of the corner of her eye with a look on her face that might have passed as a sly smile on anyone less sweet.

With that, the pair began laughing, eventually doubling over with tears streaming down their cheeks. One would begin to calm and look at the other, and they would begin all over again.

Soon their levity gave way to tiredness and they climbed into the bed and snuggled together, drifting off to sweet dreams of their beloveds.

~~~***~~~
~~~

The next morning, Darcy was up early. He broke his fast with Bingley and Colonel Fitzwilliam, the three spending the meal sharing news. He had admitted to Bingley his part in separating him from Miss Bennet, and that he had wrongly believed she did not care for him, the day after the theater outing. Bingley had been angry, but had been far more forgiving of him that he had been of his sister. In his words, "I should not have listened to either of you, but her deceit in keeping Jane's presence in London a secret from me runs far deeper than yours in attempting to convince me that she had no feelings for me. You did not know Jane was in London; Caroline did, and she kept it from me. Worse, she insulted the woman I love and to whom she was acting as a friend! What kind of person does that? I certainly do not need that in my life!"

Now that weeks had passed, Bingley was still angry with his sister, and determined to keep a distance between them. Darcy understood his feelings very well. He offered his support unconditionally.

After eating and as soon as he knew the shops would be open, Darcy went out looking for a bouquet of lavender. By the time it was acceptable to call, he had found his flowers and had bought all the shop had. He had the stems wrapped in a wide white ribbon, and held the large bunch very carefully as he exited the shop and climbed into his carriage. Telling the footman his destination, he settled in as the door was shut, maintaining his hold on the precious gift. It would not do for his Elizabeth to receive anything that was not as perfect as he could make it.

A half hour later, his arms aching a bit from his careful hold on the flowers, Darcy exited his equipage in front of the Gardiners' house. Soon, he was handing his hat and gloves to the maid who had admitted him and being announced to the family gathered in the drawing room. He was not surprised to see Bingley already there.

As he entered, a gasp went up amongst the female occupants of the room at the sight of the huge bouquet. Elizabeth's hand went up to her mouth. He was declaring to her and everyone in the room his devotion, and she could think of nothing more romantic for such a private man to do.

He soon stood before her. Bowing, he said, "These are for you, my love. I know from our discussions how fond you are of purple flowers, and I remembered that these particular ones stand for love and devotion." He smiled at her before continuing. "I wanted to surprise you with a gift, and could not think of anything I thought you might enjoy more."

As she curtseyed, then accepted the bouquet into her arms, Elizabeth graced him with a radiant smile. "Thank you, Fitzwilliam. They are beautiful! You made an excellent choice!"

"Oh, Lizzy," Aunt Gardiner gushed, "what a beautiful bunch of lavender! There are enough blooms to fill several vases … what do you say we divide them up a bit? Some for your chamber, and some for the dining and drawing rooms? I am not sure I have a vase large enough to contain them all."

Laughing, Elizabeth agreed. "Yes, Aunt, that sounds like a very good plan."

Mrs. Gardiner rang the bell for the maid before taking the bouquet. "I will be back shortly. Please, Mr. Darcy, have a seat. I will order biscuits and a fresh pot of tea while I am gone."

"Thank you, madam," Darcy replied, before seating himself on the settee next to his betrothed.

"I say, Darcy, you make it hard on a gentleman to keep up with you. I fear that I may seem to be lacking in courtship skills in comparison to to you," Bingley teased his friend, delighting in the blush that spread over his face as the ladies giggled. "First you propose before I do, then you buy every flower in London to present to your betrothed. I believe I need to get on with things; at the rate you are going, you will be back from the honeymoon before I am able to gather my thoughts."

Laughter overtook the room. Even Darcy, as much as he hated being teased, chuckled along. "Perhaps, then, my friend, you should get on with it."

"Perhaps I should," his friend replied, glancing at the object of his affections. "Perhaps I should."

Chapter 8

Lady Catherine de Bourgh was angry. Her ungrateful, disrespectful, selfish nephew had just left her house after refusing to honor the tacit agreement his mother had made with her. She had never been so insulted in her life. Then to be threatened by him; to be warned off and informed that she would be denied entrance to his homes! She had never realized he could be so discourteous to his elders. It had to be the influence of that upstart little baggage he had tied himself to. However, she had never been one to be cowed and she refused to start now. This engagement of his must be broken; the marriage must not come to pass.

Lady Catherine had reasons for insisting on a union between her daughter and the only son of her sister. Firstly, it was desired by herself and her long-dead sibling. Well, her sister had never actually said the words, but Catherine knew in her heart that her dearest Anne would agree with her. That was enough, really. If one looked further, though, if one pushed enough, there were other reasons she needed it to happen. While she did not recognize them as such, all were based in fear.

Lady Catherine had been a widow for fewer than six and thirty months. Burned into her memory, even more so than the day he died, was the reading of her husband's will. That was the day dread and anxiety had taken root in her heart.

Catherine had married Sir Lewis de Bourgh following her fourth season. She had just turned two and twenty; he was thirty. It had not been a love match, though it was not arranged, either. The two met at Almack's in

February of that year. He asked her to dance, she accepted. They continued to meet at other balls and dinners that season, and it seemed as though they always ended up paired together. They learned enough of each other by the end of April to know that they would be able to forge a life together without either being overly unhappy. So, they married at the end of May in a large, well-attended ceremony fitting for the daughter of an earl.

Over the many years of their marriage, the two had developed a fondness for each other. There was no strong passion; though neither objected to doing their duty in the marriage bed, and although it was mildly pleasant for both, sparks did not fly between them. Their hearts remained largely untouched, but as neither had ever felt anything different, they were not bothered by it overmuch.

Lady Catherine had found herself with child seven times over the course of her forty years with Sir Lewis. Four of those times had ended in miscarriage. Two of her living children had died, including the one son she had birthed. Her daughter Anne, the sickliest child she had borne, was the only one who remained. She loved Anne, as she had loved all her children. Indeed, she had been sent into deeper doldrums with every loss. Each one had been harder to draw herself out of, but she had no choice. By the time Sir Lewis was struck with apoplexy, passing away hours later, Lady Catherine had begun to build walls around her heart to protect herself from more pain. The hardness of those walls was cemented with the reading of the will.

Sir Lewis's attorney, Mr. Hastings, had traveled to Rosings from London after receiving her letter informing him of her husband's death and the need to execute his last requests. Upon his arrival, and after gathering everyone together who was required, the attorney had begun reading the words that would change her world forever.

Sir Lewis had left Rosings to Anne. The de Bourghs had not felt it necessary to entail property away from the female line, and for that, Catherine was grateful. It was what came next that caused the shock. She would lose her home upon Anne's marriage and be forced into the dower house. That was not the worst of it. Her income would be greatly reduced, to just the interest from what remained of her dowry. Not only would she be forced to move to a much smaller abode, but her funds would be cut in half. Lady Catherine had enjoyed the power that being the wife of the highest-ranking gentleman in the area gave her. Without a decent home and funds, she would become a laughing-stock.

She did not realize it, but she feared being alone and forgotten. She had spent her life being a wife, a mother, and the mistress of a grand estate. She knew no other manner of living. That fear gave way to anger, and then to bitterness. She needed to be in control of something, because she felt that her life was becoming unmanageable. Therefore, she began trumpeting as fact an engagement between Anne and the safest choice she had for a son-in-law: her nephew. Oh, she had been telling him for years that he was formed for her daughter, but never with such tenacity and desperation. Once she realized what her future held, she began insisting more strongly to Darcy that he was engaged to her daughter, and started mentioning it in front of others who were not family. She needed him to marry Anne so that she would not have to move to the dower house. As a Darcy, her daughter would live at

Pemberley, allowing Lady Catherine to remain in the home she had inhabited for longer than any other. She would lose neither status nor standing. She could not guarantee that any other arrangement would have the same happy result.

Her need for control manifested itself in other ways, as well. She had always been a woman of strong opinions and a strong personality, but she began ordering the lives of her subordinates with ferocious intensity. Of course, with her standing, none could deny her. She attempted the same with her relatives, arranging their affairs, to the extent they would allow her. Hence her loud argument with Darcy. Then, a few months after Sir Lewis's death, her rector also passed away, and she chose from among the candidates the most obsequious, easily led clergyman she could find.

All her plans now lay in ruins around

her. She did not intend for Darcy to ever marry Miss Bennet. Regardless of his words, she would see that if he did not intend to marry her daughter, he would marry no one.

After much deliberation, Lady Catherine decided the most expeditious method of removing Miss Elizabeth Bennet from her nephew's life was to approach her father. It would not do for Darcy to break the engagement; that would damage his reputation. No, the Bennet family would have to do it. She knew already that Longbourn was small, and she knew that it was entailed to her rector. What would induce him to force his daughter to give Darcy up? she wondered.

She could offer him money, of course. She considered various amounts, deciding upon a maximum limit to go along with the first bid. She was willing to negotiate, to a certain point.

Money was not the only thing she could use to entice the man into letting her nephew go. She could offer a piece of property or a house that he could set aside for his wife and daughters after he was gone. However, she did not own property in Hertfordshire and she certainly did not want Bennets living in Kent near her. No, money was the thing. No man would turn down such a generous sum as she was prepared to offer.

Once her course was decided upon, Lady Catherine wasted no time in setting out to follow it. Early the very next morning, just as the sun began to peek over the horizon, she ordered her carriage and headed for Longbourn. She instructed her coachman to go through Essex rather than take the post road to London. She would stop there on her way back; until she had made Mr. Bennet see reason, she would avoid town and her relatives there.

The roads were rutted, making for a long journey. She finally arrived at her destination in mid-afternoon, hungry, tired, and dusty, but determined to have her way. She descended from the coach in high dudgeon.

Knocking upon the door, she was greeted by what she assumed was the housekeeper. In her typical imperious manner, she demanded, "I am Lady Catherine de Bourgh. I need to speak to Mr. Bennet immediately. Take me to him."

The servant let her in, saying, "Please wait here, madam, while I see if Mr. Bennet is at home."

"No!" Lady Catherine thundered. "I will not wait. You will take me to him now. I will brook no disobedience!"

Jumping a bit at the lady's booming exclamation, Hill began sidling toward the master's book room. When the lady made to follow her and refused once again to wait, the housekeeper shrugged her shoulders and continued across the vestibule, finally knocking on his door. When he bid her enter, she opened the wooden panel, curtseyed, and announced his visitor.

"Lady Catherine de Bourgh."

The infuriated lady stormed into the book room, and Hill quietly shut the door behind her, breathing a huge sigh of relief before heading off to the kitchen to check on the cook. If she were blessed, she would not have to deal with the lady when she left.

Inside the book room, Mr. Bennet had risen to his feet when his guest entered. He was not terribly surprised to see her here; after all, Darcy had warned him she might try something. He knew before she spoke what she was about and what his response would be. He hoped, though, to find some amusement in the lady's visit. It was not often he tangled with a peer of the realm.

"Lady Catherine, it is an honor," he stated as he bowed in greeting. "Please, do be seated." He gestured to the chairs situated in front of his desk.

"I will stand. My business with you will not take so long that I need to sit. You must know why I am here."

As his visitor stood rigidly just inside his book room, Bennet smiled a little as he replied to her first sally. "You do not mind if I do, I am certain."

He took his time lowering himself into his chair, then clasped his hands together on top of the desk. "Can I get you some tea before we start?" Not giving her time to answer, he continued. "No? Well, then; yes, Lady Catherine, I am very aware of your reasons for gracing my home with your presence. My future son-in-law warned me when he asked permission to court my daughter that you would likely make such a visit."

"I am prepared to offer you ten thousand pounds to break off the understanding between your daughter and my nephew."

"Ten thousand pounds?" He drew the words out as though he were actually considering them. Finally, he shook his head. "No, I will not destroy my own daughter's happiness for any amount of money."

His adversary was enraged by this response. "His mother and I formed an engagement for our children when they were infants. I will not have that betrothal thrown away as though it were meaningless. I will give you fifteen thousand pounds. That is my last offer. I know that this insignificant estate of yours is entailed upon my rector. With this money, you could buy a house for your widow to live in upon your death."

"Madam, I repeat, I will not break Elizabeth's engagement to Mr. Darcy, nor will I insist she do so. I will not revoke my consent in any manner. My widow, should she actually outlive me, will be well-enough taken care of, not that it is any concern of yours."

"You defy me, then? You refuse to listen to reason? I see now where your trollop of a daughter learned her arts. You will regret this, Mr. Bennet, and so will all your family! I will see to it!" Lady Catherine was angrier than she had ever been.

Bennet had begun to fear she might suffer an attack of apoplexy, or something similar. However, when she began insulting his Lizzy, he reacted swiftly and strongly. His amusement was at an end. He surged to his feet.

"Lady Catherine. I have heard enough. You will not insult my daughter further. If you were a man, I would call you out! I say for the final time I will not, under any circumstances or for any reason, destroy my daughter's happiness by forcing her to break her engagement. You may be assured, madam, that before this day is over, Mr. Darcy will have been made aware of your presence in this house, your offer, and your slander of his betrothed. You will now leave my home with all due haste. You are no longer welcome at Longbourn; do not darken my doorstep again."

Bennet pointed to the door, face red and scowling, body held stiffly. In truth, he was fighting the urge to physically throw her out himself. It was only his lifetime of behaving as a gentleman that prevented him.

As if sensing he was needed, Mr. Hill,

the housekeeper's husband and Longbourn's butler, opened the door and stepped in.

"Mr. Hill, good, good! Escort this … person … out of the house immediately. She is never to be granted entrance again. Am I clear?"

"Yes, sir." He nodded, then turned to Lady Catherine, who had begun sputtering, and held his arm out towards the hallway. "After you, madam."

"You have not heard the last of me!" She angrily strode through the door, exclaiming loudly all the way to her coach.

Bennet caught part of it.

"I have never been thus treated in all my life!"

He chuckled darkly. Perhaps not, but once her nephew read his report of this incident, he was sure she would be treated far worse.

The first thing he wanted to do now was write an express to Darcy, describing his aunt's visit. The man needed to know what his mother's sister had done, and since he was not expected in Hertfordshire for at least another fortnight, Bennet thought it had best be done right away. Though not normally one to be prompt in doing anything, he knew Lizzy's protection was worth the extra effort. He wrote quickly, giving basic details and promising a more comprehensive letter to follow. Ringing for Hill, he gave her the letter and instructed her to immediately find an express rider to take it to Darcy House in London. He hoped it would reach its destination before Lady Catherine did.

Finishing that, he walked out in the garden, hoping the exercise would help to dissipate some of the residual anger he was feeling. He needed to think clearly in order to decide what, if anything, to tell his family about the visit. Thankfully, Mrs. Bennet had taken Mary, Kitty, and Lydia to visit her sister. She was unaware of what had transpired and would only know what he told her. If he were able to stress to the servants to keep quiet about it, he would not have to share any of it with her at all.

As Bennet paced, hands clasped behind his back, up and down the paths, past beds of lavender, roses, and all manner of other flowers, he began to calm. He knew that he could not count on the servants to remain quiet. He could, however, stress to them the importance of not upsetting the mistress. Everyone in the household knew how distressed Mrs. Bennet could become and the uproar such a thing caused. He was fairly certain he could convince them to at least evade her questions should one of them slip up and tell her. He nodded at this decision, heading back into the house to ask Hill to gather the servants into the kitchen.

Chapter 9

By the time Lady Catherine arrived from Longbourn to her brother's home in London, she had worked herself up into an impressive state of agitation. An average person would have been left exhausted after experiencing such an excess of emotion over such a long period of time as fifteen hours. Lady Catherine, however, was not an average person, not in her own mind and in truth, not in the mind of anyone who knew her. When she arrived at Lord Matlock's home, such was her anger that she ignored all proper behavior, opening his door without knocking, showing herself to his study, and pushing out of the way any servant trying to do his job.

Throwing the wooden panel open so hard it banged against the wall and flew back at her, she strode into the room, only to be brought up short before she could utter a single word to her brother. He was not there.

"What is the meaning of this? Where is Lord Matlock? Why did you not tell me he was not in his study?" She berated the hapless butler, Winslow, completely ignoring the fact that she had not given him a chance to inform her of her brother's whereabouts.

"I apologize, madam." He bowed before continuing. "The family is at dinner. This way, please."

Winslow turned away and began walking towards the dining room. Outwardly he was stoic, as was expected of a man in his position. Inwardly, he was seething. Pretentious, arrogant, stupid woman, he thought. Such were his ponderings that he arrived at his destination without having heard Lady Catherine and her continuous comments and complaints behind him.

Having walked quickly in his anger and

therefore arriving at the room before the lady, he opened the doors, stepped just inside, and announced her in his most somber tone before bowing and exiting. The earl and the countess looked up in surprise. They could tell from Winslow's voice that he was unhappy. That it was Lord Matlock's sister caused no amazement; she frequently was the source of distress in those lower in consequence than she. The earl rushed to stand as she entered the room.

"Henry, you must do something about Darcy! This cannot be allowed to go on! I demand you go to his house right now and put a stop to this ridiculous engagement! What are you doing?" she asked as she watched him sit back down. "Go now! This must be dealt with immediately!"

"I am eating dinner – a very late dinner. I am hungry. Nothing going on with Darcy or Anne or any of my children is dire enough that I need to interrupt a meal to deal with it. Sit and eat, and afterwards we can discuss your concerns." Lord Matlock was not at all happy to have such a pleasant meal interrupted by his harridan of a sister, and his tone of voice gave her notice that her concerns would wait until he was at leisure to consider them.

As independent and vociferous as she was, Lady Catherine was a product of her society. Ladies were subject to their male relations, in general, and her brother had been earl long enough to have gotten used to being master of his domain. She knew him well sufficiently to know that he would refuse to hear her concerns until he was ready to do so, and all the pushing, prodding, and loudly demanding she could do would be for naught. So, the great lady sat down and ate.

After the meal, the group retired to the drawing room to discuss Lady

Catherine's concerns. After her enforced period of relative silence during the meal, much of her violent anger had dissipated, but she was still determined to have her way. Lord Matlock, knowing that his sister required a firm hand, decided to make her wait a few minutes longer before taking on the issue of Darcy and his engagement. The express he had received from his second son the day before was somewhat reassuring. The young lady to whom Darcy was attached was at least a gentlewoman, and while it would have been preferable for him to marry someone with an excellent dowry, he certainly did not require one. Darcy had more money than the earl himself did, and a talent for earning more. A wife with no dowry would not be a hardship. However, Matlock knew that his sister's concern was less with this Miss Bennet's dowry and more with her own daughter. As he listened to his wife play the pianoforte, he contemplated his course of action. He believed it was wiser to let Catherine vent her spleen first. Once she had exhausted her arguments, they could be addressed one by one. He would not, however, dismiss Miss Bennet on the basis of his sister's opinion alone, which is what she was going to demand of him. As Lady Matlock finished her song and moved to re-join them, he sighed to himself and turned to his sibling.

"Well then, Catherine, tell me what it is that has you so upset today."

"Darcy, of course! Were you not listening earlier?" Lady Catherine may be required to be respectful of her brother and his station, but that did not mean she must do it meekly.

"Indeed, Sister. I do recall you interrupting a relaxing meal with my lovely spouse with some nonsense about our nephew." His tone turned hard. "Do not play games. Explain yourself and your behavior. I do not appreciate my butler being treated in so infamous a manner as you did today. Servant he may be, but he has been well-trained and does his job in an exceptional manner. Now, tell me about Darcy and what he has done that has upset you so."

Lady Catherine swallowed. She had obviously pushed too hard, too soon. However, this was important – too important to be dealt with lightly. In a calmer tone, she began again.

"Darcy informed me yesterday morning that he has engaged himself to a woman of inferior birth with no dowry and poor connections. She is a fortune hunter! My rector is cousin of some sort or other to her, and the rest of her relatives are in trade. Trade!" Lady Catherine was beginning to get worked up all over again. "She has seduced him with her arts and allurements, and made him forget what he owes to his family, what he owes to my daughter! He has been engaged to Anne since she was in her cradle, and he knows this! I remind him of it every year when he visits, and in every letter. What is he thinking?"

Lord Matlock allowed his sister to go on in this vein for a few more minutes before an expressive look from his wife gave him to understand that her patience was at an end and he should do something about his sibling.

"Enough!" He spoke sharply. "Stop at once this insistence that Darcy and Anne were meant for each other. You know very well that our sister never said any such thing. That is a fabrication that you came up with after her death, for reasons unknown to any but yourself." He raised his hand to stop Lady Catherine when she tried to interrupt. "You have always been known in the family for creating stories and swearing they were true so you could have your way. It did not work with Father and Mother, it did not work with Sir Lewis. Why you would think it would work with me is beyond my comprehension.

"I have heard from Richard; he sent me an express yesterday describing Miss Bennet to me and exclaiming over the love he sees in his cousin for this young lady. You know as well as I that Darcy does nothing, makes no decision, without careful consideration. His attachment to this Bennet girl is not the result of an impulse. I might believe that of Richard, but not Darcy." He nodded to his wife. "I intend to ask for an introduction for Audra and me to the lady. We will speak with her, as well as our nephew, and make our decision from there as to our support or lack thereof. Though," he added, looking to his boots, "really, if he is firm in his choice there is little we can do but support them. It would not do for society to discern a rift in the family.

"That being said," he stated, looking his sister directly in the eyes, "you will not cause either of them trouble. You will be polite in public to both of them. Welcoming, even. You will not speak of this fantasy of an engagement with Anne to anyone. Not to your closest friends, not to family, and definitely not to Darcy or Miss Bennet. Am I clear?"

Suddenly, a thought came to his mind. "And you are not, under any circumstances, to visit the young lady's family home and cause trouble there." When his sister startled and began to turn red, he knew it was too late for that warning. "What have you done?" he roared.

"I did what any concerned mother of a jilted daughter would do. I went to that insignificant estate she grew up on, and asked her father to force her to give Darcy up."

"And?" Lord Matlock prompted, knowing there was going to be more to the story, and that he was not going to be made happy by the revelation.

"And the man refused to listen to reason. He declined fifteen thousand pounds, saying that his widow would be well cared for should he pass before her. Fifteen thousand pounds! I know from Mr. Collins that the estate brings in very little. What man in his right mind would turn that amount of money down if he were not every bit as much a fortune hunter as his daughter?"

"Oh, I do not know, Sister. Perhaps a man who cared about his daughter's happiness? Who do you think you are to do such a thing? How would you feel if Anne had engaged herself to a member of the royal family and one of his aunts came to you and offered money to break the betrothal?"

He paused when he saw her start, but continued before she could speak. "Do not tell me that would never happen. Anything is possible. I am ashamed of you, Catherine. You have sullied the names of Fitzwilliam, Matlock, and de Bourgh with your thoughtless words and actions. At your age, one would have thought you would have learned to consider the feelings of others. It disgusts me that you are still as selfish now as you were when we were children.

"Go home to Rosings. I do not want to see or hear from you until you are ready to give up this fantasy of Darcy and Anne marrying and extend an apology to Miss Bennet's family. Honestly, at this point I am half-inclined to approve the match just to spite you." He rose, ringing the bell for a servant. When the housekeeper appeared, he asked that Lady Catherine be shown to the room kept ready for her.

"It is in your favor that you did not drag your daughter all over England with you on this misguided venture. Go upstairs and rest tonight. You will leave first thing in the morning. You will go directly home and you will stay there. Think about what you have done, Catherine, and how it reflects on yourself and your family. Think about the limitations you have placed on your daughter against all advice to the contrary. When you have come to your senses, write to me and I will visit. We will then discuss how this can be made right. Good night, Sister." With that, he extended his arm to his lady, who had risen with him, and left the room to retire to the master's chambers.

Lady Catherine, having no choice but

to obey, rose also and found her way to her suite of rooms.

Chapter 10

The next morning, after breaking his fast, Lord Matlock handed his sister into her carriage for the trip back to Rosings, warning her about her behavior and reminding her of his expectations and the consequences she would face if she failed to live up to them. He knew she was unhappy, but she would have to remain so. It is a shame, he thought, shaking his head, that Sir Lewis had to die before Catherine. She is unsuited to be left alone to run things.

Once back in the house, he went to his study and drafted a note to his nephew, asking for an audience and an introduction to Darcy's betrothed. He rang for the butler, requesting that it be delivered immediately and only into his nephew's hand.

An hour later, the butler returned with a message from Darcy. The delivery boy had found him just as he had been about to leave his house. His nephew would be available this evening for dinner, if it was acceptable. He believed he could bring Miss Bennet and her relatives, as well, as long as she had no previous engagements. Knowing his spouse had nothing planned for the evening, Matlock dashed off a message extending the suggested invitation to dinner for his nephew and the young lady. The relations business was a bit sticky. As a peer, it was not done to accept a tradesman into his home. The tradesman's wife, well … he had best check with the countess before he sent the message.

After asking his wife and discussing it with her, he decided to include Miss Bennet's aunt in the invitation. True, her husband was in trade, but the earl knew the pair would soon be family; after the wedding it would be acceptable to invite them both. Within just a few minutes more, his reply was off to be delivered.

~~~***~~~

"Good evening, Winslow." Darcy greeted the butler as he entered. "Let me introduce to you Miss Bennet and her aunt, Mrs. Gardiner."

Winslow bowed. "Good evening, Mr. Darcy, Mrs. Gardiner, Miss Bennet. If you will follow me, please."

The Matlocks' butler led the group to the drawing room, where the earl, the countess, and their eldest son had gathered before dinner, announcing the visitors and closing the door behind them after they entered.

The family stood as their guests crossed the threshold. Once the announcement was out of the way, Lord Matlock strode forward to shake
~~~

Darcy's hand.

"Darcy, so good to see you!" Turning his smiling attention to the rest of his nephew's party, he asked, "Would you be so good as to introduce me to your friends?"

"Certainly, Uncle." Gesturing to Mrs. Gardiner, he began. "May I introduce Mrs. Gardiner of Gracechurch Street? And this …" He paused to take the hand of the beautiful young lady standing beside him, tucking it into the crook of his elbow and covering it with his own. "Is my betrothed, Miss Elizabeth Bennet of Longbourn in Hertfordshire."

The ladies curtseyed to the earl. He grasped the hand of each and bowed over it, saying, "Welcome, ladies. Leave it to Darcy to find two of the most beautiful women in London to grace his arms. I did not know he had it in him; it is always the quiet ones, you know." He winked at them, causing Elizabeth to giggle and her aunt to smile.

"Indeed, Uncle," Darcy intoned. "Please stop flirting with my betrothed."

"Ah, Darcy, you take the fun out of everything." Lord Matlock laughed, before turning back to the ladies and gesturing for them to accompany him across the room to be introduced to his wife and son.

Once Elizabeth and her aunt had been presented to the countess and the viscount, everyone took a seat. Lady Matlock opened the evening's conversation by expressing her delight in meeting Darcy's intended.

"Miss Bennet, I have heard so much about you. My son Richard, Colonel Fitzwilliam …" She paused to look at Elizabeth, making sure she knew about whom she was speaking. When her guest nodded, the countess continued. "… wrote us a long letter, praising your good qualities. And of course, Darcy here added his effusions when he accepted our dinner invitation." She smiled at her nephew, who blushed, then turned back to Elizabeth, who was also red-faced.

The conversation continued, with Elizabeth and her aunt contributing effortlessly, even as the group relocated to the dining room. Lord and Lady Matlock asked probing but tactfully worded questions, with their guests giving succinct and polite answers. It was obvious that both women comported themselves well, and were able to converse on any number of subjects. Their table manners were lacking in nothing; in fact, if one did not know already that Mrs. Gardiner was the wife of a man in trade, one would have mistaken her for a gentlewoman, so graceful and refined was her behavior. Miss Bennet's comportment was exactly as the colonel had described to his parents – above reproach in every way.

After the meal, the ladies left the gentlemen to their port, walking back into the drawing room to enjoy some tea and conversation. Lady Matlock took this opportunity to probe even further into Elizabeth's background and accomplishments. The answers she received from the young lady were honest and forthright, and were delivered in a respectful way. She was not cowed, however, by dining and conversing with a countess. Lady Matlock could see a strength in the young lady that would serve her well as she faced the ton as Mrs. Darcy. The longer she spoke to Miss Bennet, the more certain she was that this girl was perfect for her nephew. She would wait to confer with her husband, but the countess was sure they would be welcoming Elizabeth to the family with open arms, despite what Lady Catherine wanted.

The separation of the sexes did not last long and soon the gentlemen rejoined the ladies. Darcy was heartened to see his aunt conversing freely with Elizabeth. He knew from speaking with his uncle in the dining room that Lord Matlock was pleased with his choice. To see his aunt so open and amiable was a good indication that she shared her husband's opinion, and that they would help his soon-to-be-wife make her way in society. He strolled to his betrothed's side, anxious to be in her company once again. He sat in the chair next to hers, smiling at her before speaking to his aunt.

"Lady Matlock, I trust you have enjoyed your visit with Miss Bennet?"

"Yes, nephew, I have. She is delightful." Lady Matlock paused to smile at Elizabeth before continuing. "You have chosen well. She will be magnificent moving amongst our society."

"Thank you, madam." Elizabeth blushed. "As long as Mr. Darcy considers me so, I will be pleased."

"I do, Elizabeth; have no fear of that." Darcy looked deep into her eyes.

"Thank you, sir." Elizabeth blushed deeper at his words, caught in his look. She stared back, soon losing all sense of her surroundings.

Lady Matlock laughed, breaking the spell that had bound the couple together and startling them into awareness. They each visibly jumped and then blushed further when they realized what had happened.

"I can see that we will need to keep an eye on the pair of you to keep you from becoming abominably rude," she teased as the pair turned even redder.

After their guests left later that evening, Lord and Lady Matlock met in their shared sitting room. This was not an unusual activity for them; they had long enjoyed a quiet cuddle on the settee after a long day. Their purpose at this time, beyond enjoying the closeness of a loving relationship, was to discuss their soon-to-be-niece.

"I like Miss Bennet a great deal, Henry," Lady Matlock began, not waiting longer to begin the discussion than it took to nestle herself in her husband's arms on the sofa.

"I do, as well. She is quick and intelligent. Not afraid to use her wit, either. She will keep Darcy on his guard, I think."

"Yes, and he needs that. Too often he believes he is right when he is not. He needs someone to check him now and then."

"As you do me, my dear Audra?" Lord Matlock replied with a smile, leaning down to kiss his beautiful wife.

Kissing him back and giggling like a young girl, Lady Matlock replied, "Indeed, Henry." Squeezing his middle tightly for a second, she continued their discussion. "I am of the opinion that we should support the union. More than that, I think we should publicly support it. Miss Bennet has not had a curtsey before the queen; as Mrs. Darcy that will be imperative, and I will sponsor her in that endeavor."

Lord Matlock smiled as he gave her a hug. How he loved watching her delineate her plans! She would have made an excellent general in the army. Her ability to see a whole, section it into pieces, and then lay out a course of action to conquer each piece never failed to amaze him. She was a formidable woman. And she was all his. He kissed her again and said, "Come, my dear, let us leave the details for tomorrow. I have a better way of spending this time with you."

With those words, he rose, pulled his smiling wife to her feet, and led her into his bedchamber.

Chapter 11

Rosings, Kent

Lady Catherine had never been so angry in her life. Even hours after reaching her home estate of Rosings, she seethed. Her brother, her very own brother, had ejected her from his home. He had accused her of shaming the family name. Her! Lady Catherine Fitzwilliam de Bourgh! Who did he think he was? She was trying to prevent Darcy from shaming them! She continued to rant in this manner, sometimes silently, sometimes loudly. Her servants and daughter tiptoed around her, fearful of her actions should they receive undue notice from her. It was not until dinner that she observed them flinching when she spoke and serving her from further away than was usual. However, it was Anne who finally gathered up enough courage to speak to her.

"Mama, what has you so flustered? I have never seen you in such a high state of agitation! Whatever can be the matter?" She spoke quietly but firmly. Her mother in this condition was a frightening thing, and while she did not want to worsen the situation, if she could amend it, she would.

"Your uncle is the matter! He told me he is ashamed of me, and sent me home like an errant schoolgirl!"

Anne's mouth fell open in shock. Shutting it up again quickly, she replied, "Ashamed? What could you have possibly done to make Uncle ashamed?"

At her daughter's question, Lady Catherine suddenly saw the events of the previous day in a new light. How was she to tell her only living child what she had done? Anne expected her mother to behave as a gentlewoman at all times, and she had not. Still, she tried to reason with herself, it was done for her protection. Drawing herself up, she replied, "I went to Hertfordshire and offered Miss Bennet's father money to break her engagement to Darcy so that he would offer for you."

Anne was astounded. "Mother! Tell me you did not! Did my cousin not tell you that I do not wish to marry him?" She could see the guilt mixed with anger on her only parent's face.

"You do not know what is best for you. I do. You will do as I say." Suddenly, Lady Catherine threw her napkin down beside her plate and stood up from the table. "Not that it matters now. Your uncle has refused to back me up. No one will force Mr. Bennet to do anything, and Darcy will marry the girl. I, however, refuse to acknowledge her. The pair of them have used us ill, Anne. They have used us very ill."

"No, they have not. I would have refused to marry my cousin, regardless of Mr. Bennet's acceptance of your bribe. Mama," she pleaded, "please listen to me. I do not want to marry Darcy. I do not want to marry anyone."

"Well, you must marry, and I do not want to lose the life I have now when you do!" Suddenly, the fears that she had not even admitted to herself came pouring out in an angry torrent. "I have no intention of living in the dower house on one thousand pounds per year. I will not lose control of this estate, nor the funds to which I am accustomed!" She stopped, appalled at her own words.

Anne begged her mother, tears beginning to overflow her eyes. "I would never force you to live anywhere but here. I do not need to marry. Even were I to meet someone and fall in love, I would not push you out of my life in that manner."

Suddenly, Lady Catherine slumped a bit, the fight going out of her for the first time since hearing of her nephew's engagement.

"You would not have a choice, my child," she stated softly. "Your father's will specifies that upon your marriage, I must move to the dower house and live off the interest from what is left of my dowry. I wanted you to marry Darcy because my sister and I agreed to it, but also because I did not want to lose my home and my income, and the benefits that come with them."

"Does the will indicate that I must marry? What happens if I do not? I know that I have inherited, as you have often said the de Bourghs did not think it necessary to entail the estate to the male line. May I not leave it to anyone I choose? And should I not marry, why can I not leave it to you, Mama, if I were to leave this mortal coil before you do?

Do you not think I would assure your health and happiness? You are my mother; I love you!"

As she spoke, Anne had crept closer to her mother, reaching out her hand, and finally grasping the one that had held hers through many a trial and tribulation. Lady Catherine squeezed her daughter's fingers tightly. Finally letting go and heaving a huge sob, she broke down in tears. Anne helped her back into her seat before sitting on the arm of the chair and wrapping her own arms around her parent. She held her mother close while Lady Catherine wept.

When the tears let up, Anne tightened her hold and spoke softly into her mother's hair. "All will be well, Mama. We will ask the attorney to come to Rosings. He can explain things to us more fully. Regardless of what the will says," she finished softly, "I cannot imagine forcing my dearest mother to live somewhere she is not happy and on little income. I trust that you will have trained me to be mistress well enough that you will be able to step back from your place and allow me mine." Letting go a little bit, she leaned back and looked her mother in the eye and smiled. "I love you, Mama."

"I love you too, Anne. Thank you for reassuring me. I am proud of you for forcing me to have this conversation. I think I needed to express my fears." She chortled. "I did not realize I felt some of those things. I needed you to draw them out of me. Thank you, Daughter."

"You are welcome. Come; let us get you upstairs. I think you could do with a long, relaxing bath. What say you?"

And so, the mistress of Rosings and her beloved daughter went upstairs together after their very trying discussion, each with a better understanding of the other and of themselves. In her bath a little while later, Lady Catherine reflected on the events leading up to that conversation. She felt an incredible amount of shame for the manner in which she had behaved, starting with her angry words to her nephew when he spoke of his engagement to Miss Bennet. Her brother was correct. She had shamed the family and cast a slur upon its name. She must make amends.

Dressing in a nightgown and robe after leaving the tub, she sat down at the table in her bedchamber and opened the small portable writing desk she kept there. She would start with letters of apology to Darcy and to her brother. Those would not be easy to write, she knew, but harder would be the ones her conscience dictated she write to Miss Bennet and her father. Some would argue that she did not directly insult the young lady, and therefore no apology was necessary. However, Lady Catherine felt convicted to write them. She had directly insulted Mr. Bennet in any case, and she had roundly derided his daughter in every conversation, not to mention attempting to interrupt the young lady's wedding.

In an effort to heal the breach between herself and Darcy and his betrothed, she issued an invitation to the pair to visit Rosings after they were married. Time would tell if this olive branch was accepted. In the meantime, Lady Catherine vowed to herself to spend part of each day reflecting on the feelings that led to her actions, in an effort to identify and conquer her remaining fears.

Chapter 12

Rosings, Kent

Lady Catherine slowly approached the stone marking her husband's grave. This was the first time she had visited in the more than three years since his death. It had been too painful; she had been too full of anger. Now, however, her pain was eased and she desired to make peace with his memory. Kneeling carefully down, she gently laid the bouquet of roses, peonies, zinnias, stonecrop, and yew greenery at the base of the marble marker. Each item in the nosegay was chosen carefully, to describe her feelings. She knew Lewis was not present to see the blooms; the symbolism was more for her than for him.

"Lewis," she whispered. "I am so sorry." Tears began tracking down her face as she started to unburden herself before him. "I allowed myself to be hardened by our losses, then failed to trust in the love of our daughter. I was so angry with you when I heard the provisions in your will. I was grasping at things that should not have mattered. I forgot what was important. I am at peace now, Lewis. I know that Anne will never leave me alone. She has said I could live with her if she marries, and she trusts me to teach her to run Rosings. I have learned that I will not lose my place.

"I am so sorry, my dear, for not trusting you and for causing such shame amongst our families. I miss you. I miss your gentle spirit and your tenderness. I love you. Thank you for giving me Anne, and for caring so greatly for me while you were here. I promise to be a better mother and to give up my role as mistress of the house when the time comes. I promise to honor you in all things. Goodbye, husband."

With that, the great lady of Rosings slowly gained her feet, wiped her eyes, and returned to the carriage that waited to deliver her back to the house.

Longbourn, Hertfordshire

Late June

The doors to the Longbourn church swung wide as the wedding guests swept out and lined the walk leading away from the building. The sound of the pianoforte preceded the newly-married Fitzwilliam and Elizabeth Darcy as they exited. The gathered relatives and friends of the couple showered them with rice, greetings, and well-wishes as they hurried into their carriage. Following, after a delay of a few minutes, came a second bridal couple – Charles and Jane Bingley – to be greeted with the same cheers and congratulations.

As soon as Darcy settled into the open-top carriage after handing his new wife in, he signaled the driver to proceed. Feeling it start to move, he reached over and took hold of Elizabeth's hand.

"At last, darling! I am beyond happy to finally give you my name and my ring. I love you." He lifted her gloved hand to his lips, bestowing a lingering kiss and reveling in the look of love in her eyes.

"And I love you, my handsome husband. I thought this day would never come! If I had to listen to Mama's effusions one more day, I would have run mad," she replied, rolling her eyes.

Darcy chuckled, thinking of the daily chaos Mrs. Bennet had created with her excitement and insistence that every aspect of the double wedding be perfect. Certainly, more than once over the course of the last six weeks his Elizabeth had rescued him from the endless, piercing exclamations of her mother.

"Do you recall, my love, the day she insisted on reviewing the menu for the wedding breakfast with me? How many times did I tell her it did not matter to me what she served?" The two laughed at the memory.

"You quickly acquiesced, though. I believe you realized the quickest way to silence her was to give her what she wanted." Elizabeth's wink caused Darcy to laugh outright, which in turn made her smile wider and squeeze his hand.

The carriage pulled up in front of Longbourn Manor and came to a stop, startling the couple out of their tete-a-tete. They disembarked quickly so their carriage could move away, allowing the Bingley equipage room to pull to the door. Once the foursome was together again, and congratulations exchanged, they entered the house to await the guests. They proceeded to the dining room, where a profusion of lavender and roses decorated the chamber, complementing the colors of the brides' dresses.

Within a few minutes, Mrs. Bennet could be heard entering the house, her shrill voice proclaiming her triumph in having two daughters so well set. She bustled into the dining room, scanning the tables and interrogating Mrs. Hill to make sure all the arrangements were complete.

Longbourn's mistress had experienced a range of emotions upon learning of the engagements of her two eldest daughters. She was overjoyed for Jane. She was completely bewildered by Lizzy's engagement. There was much she did not understand about it. Firstly, why anyone as rich as Mr. Darcy would want to marry her wildest daughter; and secondly, why Lizzy would want to marry such a proud, disagreeable man. Attempts had been made to explain these things to her, but Mrs. Bennet was of a mean understanding, and soon gave up her efforts at comprehension and instead focused on the pin money and carriages Lizzy would have.

She tried very hard to convince the couple to host the family in London for the next season, with little success. Elizabeth seemed strangely resistant to the idea. Did she not want her younger sisters to share in her good fortune? How were they to meet other rich men if she did not host them? When she took her concerns to her husband, he merely stated that what the Darcys chose to do was out of his purview. It was really quite vexing!

Well, she thought, I am sure I will have more success asking Jane. She is always obedient! I may have lost that battle, but I will win the war! And so began her campaign to sway her eldest daughter to bend to her will.

Following the Bennets into the dining room were the Gardiners. Having witnessed and supervised the reconciliation between Jane and Bingley, and approved the beginnings of the courtship of Darcy and Elizabeth, they were unsurprised at the results. They felt the girls had each made a very good match with the man who perfectly met their needs. They were pleased to have played such an important part in their nieces' lives. They had already been invited by Darcy and Elizabeth to visit Pemberley later in the summer, an offer they had every intention of accepting.

Other guests began to slowly enter.

Following her daughter and nearly the last was Darcy's Aunt Catherine. She had asked upon her arrival at Netherfield yesterday for an audience with her nephew, his betrothed, and Mr. Bennet. She had humbled herself before them, apologizing for her previous actions in attempting to prevent the marriage. Though still angry to varying degrees, the three chose to forgive her after perceiving her sincerity.

Darcy House, London

Early July

"Darling," asked Darcy as he entered his wife's dressing room, "are you certain we must attend this ball?"

The young couple had been married for just a week, and had spent every day of that time ensconced in their rooms, enjoying all the activities that married couples everywhere took pleasure in. Not all of their time was spent in bed, of course. They lounged on the sofa, cuddled together in front of the fire, reading and talking. They debated a whole host of topics, from poetry to philosophy. They discussed current events. They even shared a bath a few times. All meals were taken in their rooms; no one beyond their personal servants saw them for a se'ennight, until tonight. This night, Lady Matlock was hosting a ball in their honor. It was to be Elizabeth's introduction to society, and neither was particularly looking forward to it, other than for the opportunity to dance together.

"Yes, my love, we must. Your aunt is eager to present us as a couple, and it truly will lay the foundation for my acceptance when we return for the season next year." Elizabeth stood from her dressing table, turned, and looked at her husband with sympathy and love in her eyes. Tenderly, she asked, "Are you not eager to stand up with me for a set?"

Darcy, reaching her as she stood behind her stool, wrapped his arms around her waist and drew her to his chest. "Oh, yes, indeed I am. That is the only reason we are not in bed at this very moment. It will be months before we have another opportunity to dance together. I am eager to show you off to all my London acquaintance."

Elizabeth laughed and hugged his middle tightly. "At least those still in town, yes?"

Darcy squeezed her. "Yes, minx." Leaning down, he kissed her lingeringly. "Mmmm. You are delicious." He kissed her again, deepening it and losing himself in the feelings the activity elicited.

Elizabeth recognized the danger of continuing on the course they were heading down. "Thank you; your taste is delightful, as well, but we must discontinue before we are so distracted from our goal that we fail to attend. I would hate to disappoint your aunt. She has been so supportive of us."

Darcy sighed deeply before reluctantly responding. "I know. I am sorry. Come, Sweetheart, let us go now, before I throw you on that bed and forget all about dancing in public."

Elizabeth giggled into her hand at his words, tucking her free one into the crook of the elbow he held out to her.

Later, at Matlock House, the couple got their opportunity to dance with each other. Darcy was incredibly proud of Elizabeth. She had dazzled most everyone she had met. Her poise, wit, and good humor combined with her sparkling eyes and ready smile had endeared her to all who took the time to speak with her. Her beauty and fashionable gown in white and lavender inspired the ladies, who immediately inquired as to the name of her modiste, giving her an opening to begin conversation.

Of course, there were those who disliked her without bothering to get to know her. Some were jealous single ladies and their mothers; others were peers with set ideas about social expectations. In marrying a lady of lower consequence, Darcy had set their ideas upside down, and they did not respond well. Many understood the significance of the bouquets of dried lilac and lavender that decorated the ballroom, but it did not make a difference to them. Marrying for love was simply not done in their circles. In time, Elizabeth would win over many of these lords and ladies, but there were some who would never accept her.

None of this bothered the Darcys in the least. Each felt they had found their soulmate, and the opinions of those so wholly unrelated to them mattered not.

The End

Before you go …

If you enjoyed this book, please consider leaving a review at the store where you purchased it.

Also, consider joining my mailing list at

https://mailchi.mp/ee42ccbc6409/zoeb urtonsignup

~Zoe

About the Author

Zoe Burton first fell in love with Jane Austen's books in 2010, after seeing the 2005 version of Pride and Prejudice on television. While making her purchases of Miss Austen's novels, she discovered Jane Austen Fan Fiction; soon after that she found websites full of JAFF. Her life has never been the same. She began writing her own stories when she ran out of new ones to read.

Zoe lives in a 100-plus-year-old house in the snow-belt of Ohio with her Boxer, Jasper. She is a former Special Education Teacher, and has a passion for romance in general, Pride and Prejudice in particular, and stock car racing.

Connect with Zoe Burton

Email: zoe@zoeburton.com

Facebook:

https://www.facebook.com/ZoeBurton
Books

https://www.facebook.com/groups/Bur
tonsBabes/

Website: https://zoeburton.com

Support me at Patreon:

https://www.patreon.com/zoeburtonau
thor

Join my mailing list:

https://mailchi.mp/ee42ccbc6409/zoeb
urtonsignup

Pinterest:

https://www.pinterest.com/zoeburtona
uthor/

More by Zoe Burton

Regency Single Titles:

I Promise To...

Lilacs & Lavender

Promises Kept

Bits of Ribbon and Lace

Decisions and Consequences

Mr. Darcy's Love

Darcy's Deal

The Essence of Love

Matches Made at Netherfield

Darcy's Perfect Present

Darcy's Surprise Betrothal

To Save Elizabeth

Darcy Overhears

Merry Christmas, Mr. Darcy!

Darcy's Secret Marriage

Darcy's Christmas Compromise

Darcy's Predicament

Darcy's Uneasy Betrothal

Darcy's Yuletide Wedding

Darcy's Unwanted Bride

Darcy's Favorite

Darcy's Christmas Scheme

Mr. Darcy: The Key to Her Heart

Darcy's Happy Compromise

Darcy's Honorable Proposal

Victorian Romance:

A MUCH Later Meeting

Western Romance:

Darcy's Bodie Mine

Bundles:

Darcy's Adventures

Forced to Wed

Promises

Mr. Darcy Finds Love (available exclusively to newsletter subscribers)

The Darcy Marriage Series Books 1-3

Mr. Darcy, My Hero

Coming Together

Christmas in Meryton

The Darcy Marriage Series:

Darcy's Wife Search

Lady Catherine Impedes

Caroline's Censure

Pride & Prejudice & Racecars

Darcy's Race to Love

Georgie's Redemption

Darcy's Caution